Marsh Madness

Marsh Madness

Caroline Cousins

John F. Blair, Publisher *Winston-Salem, North Carolina*

The paper in this book meets the guidelines
for permanence and durability of the Committee on
Production Guidelines for Book Longevity
of the Council on Library Resources.

Cover Image
Photographer / Martin Tucker
Stylist / Anne Waters

Library of Congress Cataloging-in-Publication Data
Cousins, Caroline.
Marsh madness / by Caroline Cousins.
p.   cm.
ISBN-13: 978-0-89587-315-6 (hardcover : alk. paper)
ISBN-10: 0-89587-315-X (hardcover : alk. paper)
ISBN-13: 978-0-89587-309-5 (pbk. : alk. paper)
ISBN-10: 0-89587-309-5 (pbk. : alk. paper)
1. Women detectives—South Carolina—Fiction. 2. Plantation life—Fiction. 3. South
Carolina—Fiction. 4. Weddings—Fiction. 5. Cousins—Fiction.
6. Islands—Fiction. I. Title.
PS3603.0888M37 2005
813'.6—dc22   2005005228

Design by Debra Long Hampton

For the family—again—
and in memory of our grandmothers:

Georgia Godwin Pate Bridge
Beulah Hiott Kinsey Love
Margaret Gohagan Godwin

Marsh Madness

Prologue

On the night of the vernal equinox, lightning split the inky sky as a spring storm rushed down the river to the sea. Thunder boomed across the island. Wind whipped the Spanish moss hanging from gnarled oaks, tore at dead limbs and dry palmetto fronds. Rain drenched woods and marsh, thrumming the tin roof of the big, empty house.

The house had seen much worse over the years, including a hurricane with no name that blew away one beach and formed another. That storm also cleaved a smaller barrier island from the old. It shifted sand, sank ships, uprooted trees, destroyed homes and hopes. People died.

This storm ended as quickly as it began, with a final flurry of rain over a tidal creek where cypress stumps reached skyward. A last flash of lightning illuminated a large silver log embedded in the oozing mud.

Was it the wind, or maybe just a shadow from that burst of brightness? Did the log move?

Chapter One

Pinckney Purple Rides Again

At exactly four o'clock in the afternoon on the last Monday in March, the double mahogany doors opened wide.

"Welcome to Pinckney Plantation."

My cousin Margaret Ann stopped dead in her tracks on the brick path leading to the wide front porch. "Lindsey Lee Fox, what in the world have you got on your head?"

"Don't you like it?" I said, preening. "I found it in a box in the room where we keep the tour-guide costumes. Maybe I can wear it as an Easter bonnet this Sunday." I took off the black turban with a glittering rhinestone the size of an egg at its center. "I could pretend I'm Gloria Swanson in *Sunset Boulevard*. Do you think I'm ready for my closeup?"

"For Halloween," said Margaret Ann. "Honestly, Lindsey, if you don't have anything better to do than play dress-up in the storage closet, I have a whole list of things here that need doing for Sue Beth's wedding." She waved a sheaf of papers at me. "Besides, Miss Augusta would have a dying-duck fit if she knew you were opening the front door in that getup. What if I had been a group of tourists?"

"We're closed on Monday," I reminded her, standing at the top of the steps. "And it's not like I couldn't see you coming through the parlor window. And furthermore, Miss Augusta's not going to know 'cause she's too busy playing bingo at Bayview. It's part of the amenities at 'the Low Country's newest and most luxurious senior-care village.' "

"Somehow, I don't picture Augusta Pinckney Townsend of Indigo Island playing bingo at a rest home, even if it is Bayview. She's been there only two weeks, and she's still organizing things more to her liking."

I looked out at the curving drive beneath an arch of ancient oaks draped with Spanish moss, a picture-postcard view that practically shouted "Old South." Margaret Ann was busy rummaging in her large leather shoulder bag for something.

"Here," she said, handing over an envelope. "Miss Augusta asked me to give you this. It's a list of things she wants from Pinckney. It's all little stuff except for that lamp from her bedside and one of the tea sets. She said there's a nice English rose one in the attic."

The attic. Oh, great. The last time Margaret Ann and I had tea with Miss Augusta, we'd ended up locked in the attic at Pinckney and then had to go to the ER. That was right after New Year's, and only a few days after we'd discovered a body at the foot of those same narrow attic stairs.

"I'll take the lamp when I go see her tomorrow," I said. "Maybe she'll forget about the tea set by then."

"Don't count on it. Miss Augusta's getting more like her old self every day. You can hardly tell she had that stroke—if that's what it was—except for the walker. I wouldn't wonder if she ran out of rehab once she heard that corner suite at Bayview is available. It's really quite the showplace of rest homes. Their azaleas don't look as good as these, though." Having recently started a special-event floral business, Margaret Ann appraised the pink blossoms with an expert eye. The buds had flowered dramatically this week in the wake of spring showers. "They should be at their peak for the reception." She looked at me critically. "You're a mess, though. I hope you're planning to change before we go to the Gatortorium."

"Sorry I don't fit your idea of management," I said. "If you'd been here at the crack of dawn to meet the cleaning crew, the landscapers, the security consultant, and the termite guy—although he didn't show up—you might not look so good yourself. Plus, I had to go through all the guide costumes to see which ones need mending, so Marietta could take them home."

Although Pinckney's longtime housekeeper was in her eighties, as was Miss Augusta, she claimed to still have twenty-twenty vision. Marietta knew if a speck of dust settled anywhere in the downstairs rooms of the old plantation house that were open to the public. She complained often about the group of women who came early in the mornings armed with mops, buckets, and an arsenal of aerosols. "They clean round," she grumbled. "Don't none of 'em know what a corner is."

Margaret Ann brushed off my complaints like they were a cloud of gnats. "At least you don't have to listen to Beth. I know she's the mother of the bride and my good friend, but she may not be by the time this wedding is over." She brandished a stack of pink while-you-were-out messages. I recognized the curlicue writing of Margaret Ann's teenage daughter, Cissy. "I'm trying to stay professional about this, but Beth is 'bout to drive me crazy. You're going to help me, aren't you?"

"Yes, Mam," I saluted with a grin. Margaret Ann's been called "Mam" since forever on account of her initials. She was a Mikell before she married J. T. Conveniently, his last name was Matthews. "And Bonnie's in the kitchen. They dropped her off on the way out of town."

They were our respective parents, who were taking Bonnie's two little boys to Disney World for spring break while her Navy husband was out in the Atlantic somewhere.

"Good Lord." Mam headed for Pinckney's front door. "I hope she hasn't found those *petits fours* in the freezer or there won't be enough for the reception."

"Oh, come on," I said. "You're just jealous because your little sister can eat what she wants and not gain a pound. I know I am. I think she just went to see if Marietta's still here."

"Marietta's biscuits are more like it." She marched into the hall-way, calling to me over her shoulder, "Are you coming? We need to be leaving for the Gatortorium pretty soon, and you said you're going to change your clothes."

I hadn't said any such thing, but I actually *was* planning to put on a clean shirt with some good jeans in honor of Indigo Island's newest tourist attraction's preview opening party. No way, though, was I wearing my new khakis to a pig pickin'. I'd be a magnet for barbecue sauce.

"Be there in a sec," I called to her disappearing back. "There's something I need to take care of."

The white van that had rolled up the drive boasted a plastic palmetto bug the size of a Rottweiler attached to its roof. As if there was any doubt as to its business, a magnetic sign spelled out "Hired Killers Pest Control" in black on the van's door.

"Lonnie Williams," said the beefy young guy who was about to bust the buttons of his pinstriped uniform shirt. "I'm the new bug man."

"Lindsey Fox, acting manager," I said. "I thought you were coming this morning. There's no time for you to do the inside spraying today, and you really need to get with Posey Smalls, the groundskeeper, about the outside and the other buildings."

"I know. I'm real sorry. I got tied up with a nest of wasps over at Palmetto Point. I figured I'd drive over here and apologize in person, and then that way we could reschedule." Taking off his baseball cap to reveal a receding sandy red hairline, he mopped his freckled brow. He looked like an earnest puppy dog. "Do you think if I came first thing in the morning it'd be all right? I need to inspect for termites, too. They've been swarming. Maybe you've seen little tunnels of what looked like dried mud? Could be subterraneans." He sounded hopeful.

"No," I said. "But I haven't really thought about it." Who had time for termites when tourists were swarming south in search of warm weather?

"Can't be too careful." Lonnie picked up a clipboard from the van's front seat. "There was a plantation down near Jacksonville that had to close completely for a couple of months 'cause the termites had about eaten it up. They just love old wood."

He looked with satisfaction at Pinckney. Considering that it was heading toward a bicentennial before too long, the termites would find it a fine feast. Not that there was a shortage of old wood on Indigo. Unlike its big sister Edisto Island across the river, our island on St. Helena Sound could claim only one plantation that had weathered war and hurricanes—and apparently voracious insects. But smaller houses and the ruins of other buildings that dated back to before the Civil War—some even to the Revolution—were tucked in among Indigo's stands of oaks and pines, palmettos and pecans. In fact, I was temporarily living in one, Middle House, while its owner, Miss Maudie, spent time with her son in Centerville, the county seat twenty miles inland. I wondered if Middle House had termites along with its mice in the attic and raccoons on the roof. Maybe I'd see whether Lonnie the Hired Killer could check it out, too. But first things first.

"Posey's gone for the day," I said. Lonnie's face drooped, making him look even more like a puppy, one that had just been told he wasn't allowed on the sofa. "But wait, are you going to the Gatortorium thing tonight? Posey's going to be there."

Lonnie's face brightened. "Yes'm. I'll ask for him there. Mr. Posey Smalls. Thank you very much. It's a pleasure meeting you, ma'am."

I nodded. Since I'd moved back to the island two months ago, I was getting used to being called "ma'am." Part of it was just good manners. But part of it was also people mixing up me and Mam. Not only were our mothers sisters, but our fathers were first cousins.

"We're not double first cousins, though," Mam always told people. "More like one and a half. Our mamas married first cousins. Not their own first cousins, though, so it's legal."

Despite our shared gene pool, we don't look much alike. My hair is darker, and Mam's legs are slightly longer. I have green eyes; hers are blue. But we're almost exactly the same age, Mam having arrived less than forty-eight hours after me.

"I stole your thunder," she'd say, laughing.

"Yes," I'd reply. "You're definitely the loud one."

We all have voices that carry, but Mam's carries the farthest. I heard her now as I walked into the kitchen, which unlike the rest of the downstairs has been brought into the twenty-first century and is off-limits to tourists. She was on the phone.

"No, I'll ask J. T. and just write you a check when I come tomorrow," she said. " 'Preciate you telling me, though. See you in the morning." She hung up but didn't pause for a second. "That is so weird. The wholesaler in Charleston said my credit card wouldn't go through for those flowers I just ordered for the wedding. I'm sure J. T. paid that bill, but remind me to ask him about it tonight. Now, where was I?"

"You were telling me why you need a dozen brandy snifters for the wedding," said Bonnie. She was wiping biscuit crumbs from her chin and didn't see Mam mouth an "I told you so" at me.

I grinned back. Sitting there in her Levi's, her tousled hair falling out of a ponytail, Bonnie hardly looked like a high-priced D.C. attorney specializing in environmental law. Not for the first time, I thought it really wasn't fair, Bonnie being taller, thinner, three years younger, and blonde to boot.

"Aren't the snifters for candles?" she asked.

"No," said Mam. "This is a special request. Sue Beth's insisting on a beach wedding, and she's checked the tide charts, and it will be low tide about six on Saturday. If it doesn't rain, it should be nice then—not too hot, and the sun going down, and hopefully no bugs like later on when the no-see-ums get so bad. Course, if it does rain, we're going to have to move everything over to the Pinckney chapel, not that there's room for everybody she's invited."

"Mam," Bonnie said. "The brandy snifters?"

"The bridesmaids are going to carry them."

"Go on," I prodded. "Are they going to be full of brandy?"

"Of course not," Mam said. "The Chesnuts don't drink. This is an alcohol-free wedding. Even the champagne fountain isn't for champagne but that sparkling cider stuff. Besides, brandy would kill the fish."

"Fish?" Bonnie said. "What fish?"

"The goldfish," Mam said. "The bridesmaids are each going to carry one. I bought them from GoodPet in Centerville. Why are y'all looking like that? I'll tie ribbons on the stems—ocean blue, naturally—and they'll dangle down like bouquets. The groomsmen will wear leis made of Dendrobium orchids, and the girls will have orchids in their hair. It should be pretty."

Bonnie's laugh came out a snort.

"Okay," Mam acknowledged with a smile. "I guess it is a little over the top."

"Mercy!" Bonnie said. "It's a lot over the top. Is the reception here at Pinckney going to be a plantation luau?"

"Oh, no," Mam said. "That part's real traditional. We'll have the white tents and the chandeliers in the trees, hydrangeas and roses everywhere. Sue Beth wants the whole shebang."

"It must be going to cost a fortune," Bonnie said. "I didn't know the Chesnuts had that kind of money."

"They don't." I was looking at the guide schedule on the refrigerator to make sure Cissy was down for tomorrow, so I could go to Centerville. "But Sue Beth's grandmother left her a dining-room suite—"

"And Beth saw one like it on *Antiques Roadshow*," Mam cut in. "They had it appraised, and it was worth a lot, too, and so Sue Beth decided to sell it and use the money for the wedding. Said she thought it was ugly, and she'd rather have Pier One. Beth had a fit, being head of the historical society now, but the old lady had in her will that it was Sue Beth's, so this wedding is coming courtesy of a table and chairs."

"Okay, so answer me this," Bonnie said. "What shoes is everybody wearing on the beach? Flip-flops?"

"No, the guys can just wear regular shoes. The sand's packed tight up there at the Point." Mam scrunched her face over something on the ever-growing list of things to do for the wedding.

Mam had her own code, so I never knew if some hieroglyph on her list referred to cake or corsages. Not that I was all that interested. My own wedding had been held in a Massachusetts courtroom after the groom and I finished our summer-camp counseling jobs before my junior year in college. The ink was hardly dry on the license before I knew that marrying on the rebound was not my best idea, and I was back in Chapel Hill in time for second semester, even as Mam was showing off the diamond J. T. had given her for Christmas. I'd been in their wedding the next year, and a few others since then—and had a closetful of gosh-awful bridesmaid's dresses to prove it—but my natural romanticism was tempered by a cynicism that had come with time and experience. I'd seen too many never-used fondue sets and blenders at yard sales, too many wedding dresses in consignment shops, and, when I was working as a reporter at the TV station in Charlotte, too many domestic disputes between people who looked up one day from the bills and diapers and realized they'd married a stranger.

"My sandals have heels," Bonnie said.

"Clunky or pointed?" Mam didn't look up. "Pointed won't work. I think Sue Beth is wearing flip-flops or maybe even going barefoot. Her dress is long, so no one will see, but it still doesn't seem proper. At least the bridesmaids are wearing ballerina flats dyed to match their dresses."

"What color?" Bonnie asked.

Mam and I exchanged glances.

"Oh, don't tell me. They're not . . ." Bonnie buried her face in her arms in mock despair.

"They are," I said, having had the same reaction when Mam first told me that Sue Beth's bridesmaids would be decked out in tea-length dresses the same deep lavender as the material Miss Augusta had bought in bulk on sale at Wal-Mart for the tour-guide costumes.

"Pinckney purple rides again," Mam said. "At least they're not wearing hoop skirts."

"Oh, I don't know," Bonnie said. "Once you've got goldfish, you might as well go the whole nine yards and have that Tommy-Bahama-meets-Scarlett-O'Hara look. La! And a barefoot bride. It's all just too tacky for words. I would have thought Beth—"

She was interrupted when the back door suddenly opened and a disheveled Beth Chesnut practically fell into the kitchen.

"Oh, Margaret Ann, thank heavens you're here!" Beth's normally smooth cap of light brown hair looked like it hadn't seen a comb in days, and her mascara obviously wasn't waterproof. "The wedding will be ruined, just ruined!" She clasped her hands to her chest in a gesture that would have done a B-movie actress proud. "I could just kill MaryMar!"

CHAPTER TWO

Tastes Like Chicken

"What's a MaryMar?" asked Bonnie. "Sounds like a Girl Scout cookie."

Mam gave her an exasperated look. "Bonnie, can't you stop thinking about food for one minute? Here, Beth honey, you sit down and get yourself together, and then you can tell me all about it." She patted Beth's shoulder. "I'm sure everything's going to be just fine. Lindsey, go get some Kleenex out the hall bathroom."

Bonnie followed me out of the kitchen. "I wasn't trying to be funny," she said. "What's a MaryMar?"

"Not a what, a who," I said. I could hear Beth's sobs as I grabbed a handful of tissue. "Mary Martha Futch, only she goes by MaryMar now. It's her stage name, like Cher." Beth's crying gained momentum. "We might as well take the whole box. I'll tell you more later, but I want to hear this first."

Mam poured water from a plastic Deer Park jug into a jelly glass and handed it to Beth. I slid over the Kleenex.

"Just sip that slowly." Mam's voice was soothing, almost hypnotic. It was the same tone she used to talk Cissy out of teenage tantrums and J. T. out of a tiz when he couldn't find the keys to his truck. Apparently, it was quite handy with nervous-nelly brides and their ready-to-snap mothers, too.

"I'm sorry," Beth said. "I didn't mean to dump all this on you, but I was so mad when I heard." Her bottom lip trembled. "I mean, it's just so inconsiderate. Sue Beth asked her months ago, her being Wiley's second cousin on his daddy's side. But we never dreamed . . . I mean, she's gotten so big for her britches being in those car commercials that she hardly ever comes here. And now, to just suddenly up and decide she wants to be in the wedding after all . . ."

"So MaryMar *is* going to be a bridesmaid." Mam sat down at the table across from Beth and picked up a pencil. "That's not a problem, really. We've still got five days. Let's see. We'll need another grooms-man, but it seems like half of Clemson and Carolina is down here or at Edisto for spring break. I'm sure we can draft a fraternity brother who's got a dark suit or can borrow one." She made a notation and contin-ued. "There's going to be enough food to feed an army. I'll pick up extra flowers. And an extra fish. Maybe two, just to be on the safe side." I didn't dare look at Bonnie. "Now, we'll need to call Lucille and see if she can work in another hair appointment Saturday morning."

"MaryMar won't need Lucille," Beth said with a hiccup. She dabbed her eyes, further streaking her mascara. "She has a friend of hers from high school who's some kind of personal assistant who does hair, too."

"Good." Mam made another mark. "Now, there's plenty of mate-rial left—I was even going to drape some on the cake table—and Marietta can whip up another dress in no time. I assume MaryMar is here now, or will be soon, so we can get her measurements?"

Beth nodded. "She'll be at the Gatortorium tonight." She blew her nose. "Turner Hickey hired her for a modeling job at the party."

"Is she wearing Pinckney purple?" Bonnie asked.

"Oh, no," Beth said seriously. "That's for the wedding. No, I'm not sure what she'll have on, other than a snake."

~

"A snake!" Bonnie shuddered in the car seat beside me. "You

wouldn't catch me wearing any snakes. I can hardly stand to look at them, although I'm not as bad as Mam. She's almost as phobic about them as you are about spiders. I can't believe she's even going tonight."

"Public relations," I said. "This is an all-island thing, and she'll network like crazy, handing out her Coming Up Roses business cards." I turned the CR-V onto King's Road. "Besides, she made me and J. T. promise to shield her from the snakes."

Bonnie had elected to ride with me to the party after Mam realized her van was still full of the wilting flower arrangements she'd collected from Bayview and the Centerville dentist's office earlier in the day, having substituted another week's worth of fresh floral designs. Now, Mam was by herself behind us, her air conditioner on full blast as she tried to dispel what Bonnie called "eau de funeral flowers."

We rolled down the windows of the CR-V to catch a breeze that smelled of salt and marsh and green growing things. Spring was flashing by as I drove, bright new leaves in the trees and tangled underbrush, dogwoods mixed in like white confetti. A burst of fuchsia announced an errant azalea by the side of an old fence bowed by sprawling kudzu and wisteria. After a colder and wetter winter than usual, the weather had suddenly turned warm, although, it being March, it could change overnight. But there was a sweetness in the air now, melding with the smell of damp earth and the sharp tang of the sea. Flocks of high-flying birds on their way north pinwheeled in the afternoon sky.

"The boys love snakes, of course," Bonnie said. "Do you think I'm a bad mother for sending off my children?"

"Are you kidding? To Orlando? They'll love it. They're going to be spoiled rotten by the time they come back."

"I know. Lieutenant Commander Tom Tyler can straighten them out next week. Meanwhile, I told them they better behave or I'd sell them on eBay." She adjusted the windshield visor so the lowering sun wouldn't be in her eyes. Seeing the mirror, she reached for her Vera Bradley purse and makeup kit. I noticed dark circles under her eyes. "I'm just tired," she said, taking out a tube of concealer. "I think I've about decided that this Superwoman needs to discard her cape for a while. I'm going to use this vacation to think about taking advantage of the firm's mommy track. Or at least I'll take the summer off while Tom's out on cruise. Maybe I'll rent a place down here for me and the boys."

I was surprised. Bonnie always seemed to balance career and family with ease. "What about the case with the artificial reefs and the old tires? Aren't you still working on that?"

"It's about wrapped up, and thank heavens I'm not involved with that case about lead in the D.C. water. Beach water may not taste good, but at least it's not poisoning you, although Mama says it's eaten away her dishwasher rack."

"I wouldn't know," I said. "Middle House is stuck back in the Middle Ages. The only dishwasher there is me."

"But you still like living there?"

"It suits me for now," I said. "I'm basically just living in the front bedroom and living room. There's no central heat, remember? Right after I moved in, we had that cold snap, and I swear my toothpaste froze."

"Like at Nanny's." Our late grandmother's house had been of similar drafty design. "Oh, Lordy, those were the coldest toilet seats. That's when I wished I was a boy." Bonnie brushed some blush on her cheeks. "So what's the deal with this MaryMar character? How come I don't remember her?"

"Probably because her family moved to Centerville when she was little. And she was behind you in school maybe four or five years," I said. "She was in the Granville County beauty pageant, though, that year they had to call the fire department."

"When that girl missed catching the flaming baton? Was that MaryMar?"

"No, that was her friend Lorna." I slowed as we rounded a bend. The turnoff for Cottonmouth Creek was just before the drawbridge, which was the only access to Indigo Island other than by boat. I saw brake lights ahead, which indicated the bridge was open for some yacht coming through the Dawhoo Cut on the Intracoastal Waterway. "MaryMar wanted to be an actress even then. She gave a dramatic reading from *Antigone*. Miss Augusta coached her, but she might as well have been speaking Greek for all the audience understood. The only reason she finished in the top five was 'cause she wore some flimsy costume that was cut down to her bellybutton."

"Oh, I think I remember her," Bonnie said. "Lots of blond hair. Is my lipstick on straight?"

"Yes, that color's good on you. But you don't need any more mascara. You better wait till I stop this car or you're liable to poke your eye out."

"Pooh," said Bonnie. "I don't have dark eyelashes like you and Mam. I'm a natural blonde, like MaryMar."

"Natural Instincts by Clairol is more like it, at least in MaryMar's case," I said. "It's practically platinum, or at least it was in the commercials."

"What commercials? I thought I heard Beth say something about MaryMar being too big for her britches."

"More like her bra," I said. "You know those TV ads for Ron Simmons, Used Car King of the Carolinas? They've been on a couple of years now."

"Do they have a chimp?"

"No, a dog," I said. "He's this cute Wheaten terrier mix, looks sort of like a big Benji, only he has one ear that sticks up and one that flops over."

"Oh, that dog is so cute! I remember seeing him on TV the last time I was here."

I braked again. Traffic was backed up about a quarter-mile, and I could see a sheriff's cruiser up near the Gatortorium entrance, where a deputy was directing traffic. "Do you remember the woman holding him?"

"No, just the dog."

"Well, that was the problem, leastways for MaryMar. She found out that Watson—that's the dog, I did a freelance piece on him for *Perfect Pet* magazine last month—was being paid more than she was. She had herself a little hissy fit and told Ron Simmons it was either her or the dog. Well, Watson's still on TV, and now MaryMar is down here wearing snakes, so you can draw your own conclusions."

⁓

"Where's MaryMar?" Mam asked nervously as she joined us. "I really don't want to see any snakes if I can help it."

"She's back over there somewhere," Bonnie reported. "I saw her when I went to get us something to drink. What do you suppose this stuff is, anyway?" She handed Mam a plastic cup filled with purple liquid. "It looks like what we used to drink in college. What was it they mixed with grape Kool-Aid? Vodka?"

"More likely Everclear," I said.

"And then there was gin and lemonade," Mam said. She shook her head at the memory. "I was such a good little Baptist girl until I went off and was corrupted by Citadel cadets. My stomach can't hack that stuff now. I think this is just Gatorade, in honor of the Gatortorium. The purple one's called Riptide Rush." She took a sip and nodded. "I wish I'd thought to bring a Coke like Lindsey, although there's probably tea and beer with the barbecue. And that's where I told J. T. I'd meet him. I just hope it's not near MaryMar and that snake."

"This way." Bonnie led us across the gravel. They pitched their empty cups into a dark green trash barrel, and I added my Coke can. "Lindsey and I'll protect you. How do you feel about alligators? The reason I'm asking is, that sign there is pointing us toward the gator ponds. But it's also where I think the food is. I don't suppose gator's on the menu."

"Could be, but I'm not eating anything but barbecue from Allgood's," I said. "They're doing the catering. I saw the van."

"I've eaten alligator before in Florida by mistake, thinking it was chicken tenders," Bonnie said. She sniffed the air. "Tastes like chicken, sort of."

"Gross," said Mam. Her eyes darted from one side of the leafy path to the other, as if a stray snake might be foolhardy enough to venture into a crowd of humans. "I'm not overly fond of gators, but they don't give me the willies like snakes. We don't have any gators in Fishing Creek that I know of, but every now and then when we take the boat up here toward Cottonmouth, we'll see a couple sunning themselves on the shore. And J. T. says there are some in that swampy area of Pinckney. They like fresh water. Brackish water is okay, but not salt water. But there was one on Front Beach last month, not too far from Aunt Mary Ann and Uncle Lee's. Did they see it, Lindsey?"

"You bet," I said. "Will had to go down there and keep people away until Turner Hickey and his assistant came. They got it in the back of a truck somehow and relocated it up here. It was only about six feet—a teenager, really, Turner said."

"Speaking of Will, why isn't Major McLeod here?" Bonnie steered us in the direction of the picnic tables. "The last Mam said, you were still dating the lawman."

"He's at some conference upstate," I said. "Something to do with the war on drugs. 'Just Say No' isn't working too well in the rural counties, at least not where crystal meth's concerned. He's coming back later this week."

"And?" Bonnie asked.

"And nothing." Mam pursed her lips. "At least that's all our dear cousin ever says when I ask her about Will. She's like one of those snapping turtles that's not going to open its mouth till it thunders."

"Did I hear something about turtles?" Turner Hickey, the proud proprietor of the Gatortorium, stood where the path forked. He was one of those weather-beaten men who could be anywhere between fifty and seventy, with jug ears, a bald head, and a smile that stretched from here to Sunday. "We've got some nice turtles in the reptile house that I know you ladies will want to see. And that's where we've put all the poisonous snakes and exotics—copperheads, corals, pythons, rattlers, moccasins, a real pretty boa constrictor I got off a boy from Beaufort. The next tour is in about fifteen minutes. But while you're waiting, look over here at this pit. Now, isn't that something?"

I heard Mam gasp. She was holding onto my forearm for dear life. I'd probably have bruises tomorrow. And I might have nightmares tonight. The trees lifting their limbs skyward from the vast concrete bowl were full of blacksnakes, twining like vines in some places, hanging like ropes in others. Medusa had nothing on this place.

"Are they dead?" Bonnie asked. She took a step toward the net and peered cautiously downward. Mam moved behind me.

"No, no. They're just a tad sluggish 'cause we hauled them out of hibernation a little early," Turner said. He kicked the netting with a brown alligator boot that looked custom-made. I hated to think of its original owner. "They'll perk up as the weather gets warmer, start slipping and sliding all around. That's when we'll post summer feeding times for the big snakes and the gators."

My stomach did a flip. If anything, Mam's clench on my arm became even tighter. "Excuse us, Turner," she said, her voice pitched a little high. "We were on our way to the ladies' room. Is it this way?"

"Do you really have to go?" I followed Mam down the left path, Bonnie trailing behind.

"Not especially," she said. "But I had to get away from there. And you looked like you might throw up."

"How could you tell? Your eyes were closed."

" 'Cause I know how squeamish you are," she said. "You've looked pale ever since Bonnie talked about eating alligator."

"I told you," Bonnie said. "Tastes like chicken. As long as we're here, we might as well use the facilities."

The wooden signs on the concrete building painted lima-bean green indicated men to the left, women to the right. Inside, three stalls faced three sinks. The middle stall was taken.

"I'll wait," I said. I took my brush out of the black book bag that doubled as my purse. Maybe I could do something with my hair.

"You can tell this place is new," Bonnie said. "There's no hook on the door. I don't want to put my good pocketbook on the floor. This tile doesn't look too clean."

"Hang it round your neck," Mam advised. "That's what I always do at the DixieMart on the way to Centerville. Drat, there's no toilet paper in here. Any out there, Lindsey?"

"No, not even paper towels, just hand dryers," I said. "I might have some Kleenex."

"Here." Bonnie's hand appeared from underneath her stall door. "Carry her this, Lindsey."

I had to bend to get the toilet-paper roll from Bonnie. The white high-heel sandals in the middle stall caught my eye. I cringed. I'd have to wait until we were outside to tell them. None of us would be caught dead wearing white after Labor Day and before Easter. Of course, Easter was this coming Sunday, and they *were* cute shoes. I bent and peeked again. What the heck? "Ma'am, are you all right?" I knocked on the stall door.

"Of course I am," Mam said, "now that I have toilet paper."

"I wasn't talking to you. I think this woman next to you might be sick or something. Her feet look funny."

"What did you say?" asked Bonnie. "Tell me before I flush."

"I said I think there's something wrong with this woman in the middle. But the doors are so long I can't really tell." I knocked on the stall door again. "You in there, are you okay?"

"Wait," Bonnie said. There was the sound of flushing from both sides. "Oh, Lordy!"

I looked up. Bonnie had climbed on top of the toilet seat and was leaning over the top of the stall looking down at Miss White Sandals.

"What is it? Who is it?" Margaret Ann's head popped up, too. She flailed one arm, trying to see from behind her shoulder bag while holding onto the top of the stall divider. "Mercy! Lindsey, slither under that door right this minute and see if she's dead. Maybe a snake bit her."

"What snake?" No way did I want to crawl around on that tile. There might really be a snake, or blood, or some sort of goo.

"Lindsey, get a grip!" Mam barked. "Don't you even think about being sick. Oh, that poor girl. Watch out, Bonnie, you're going to strangle yourself on your purse strap."

I took a deep breath and got on my knees, then gingerly lowered myself to the tile, pushing forward with my forearms until my head was under the door. I was eye level with the white sandals. The woman's toenails were painted an iridescent blue, and she was wearing a thin bracelet on one bony ankle. I looked up. All I could see was a lot of white-blonde hair cascading onto denim capris.

"It's MaryMar, isn't it?" Bonnie said. "Tell me she's not dead."

I used the toilet-paper dispenser to haul myself to my feet, then tried to sit up the slumping figure. "It's not MaryMar," I said. The blond hair had parted enough to reveal an unfamiliar, angular face sheened with perspiration. "And she's not dead."

CHAPTER THREE

Punch Drunk

"Dead drunk is more like it," Bonnie said. She waved her hand. "Yo ho ho and a bottle of rum."

She and Margaret Ann shouldered me out of the way to get a look at the young woman passed out on the commode.

"Look, there's plenty of toilet paper in here," Mam said. "She could have given me some."

"If she wasn't drunk," Bonnie said. She took a wad of tissue from the dispenser and handed it to me. "Here, Lindsey, go put some water on this, and let's see if we can get her awake enough to get her out of this stall. There's not enough room in here to swing a cat. If she's not MaryMar, who is she?"

"I don't know," I said. I handed over the damp tissue to Bonnie, who passed it to Mam, who dabbed the woman's face, crooning gently. "There, there," she said. "Come on, sugar, time to wake up."

The woman gave a little moan. Her white-blond hair was streaked dark with sweat, and the smattering of freckles on her prominent nose stood out in sharp relief to her marshmallow skin. What makeup she'd been wearing was mostly gone, although a tell-tale orange line smudged her jaw near one ear.

" "I don't know her either," Mam said. "She must be from off."

Meaning off the island. If it had been anybody but Margaret Ann telling me the woman didn't live on Indigo, I might have questioned them. But except for her college years, Mam has lived on the island her whole life and knows everybody, from the several hundred people who call Indigo home to another couple thousand who have summer or weekend houses. I was always surprised at how many new faces I saw among the familiar ones, but Mam knew them all, from the urologist from Greenville and his la-di-da trophy wife to the stock boy at the Piggly Wiggly who she had in first grade when she was still teaching.

"Here's her purse," Bonnie said, picking up a white vinyl hobo bag from the tile. Obviously, the woman was in no condition to care whether it got dirty. "Should we look in it?"

"Of course," Mam said. "How else are we going to know who she is?"

"Lorna Spivey," Bonnie pronounced. "It's a South Carolina driver's license. Says she lives in Charleston and she's—let me do the math— thirty, no thirty-one years old. I thought she might be older. She's got that rode-hard-put-up-wet look, even in this picture. Didn't you say MaryMar had a friend named Lorna?"

I took the wallet—a beaded white novelty item boasting "Fun Girl" in squiggly pink script—from Bonnie so I could see for myself the small face behind the plastic window.

"Hardly anyone looks good in their driver's license picture," Mam said over my shoulder. "I think they take a course so they can catch you cross-eyed or with your mouth open."

"I think this is MaryMar's friend, only that Lorna had a different last name, and her hair was brown," I said. "She's about the right age, though."

"How many Lornas do you know?" Bonnie asked. "Spivey must be her married name, and she most likely dyes her hair. She's MaryMar's friend, I'm sure of it." She held up a key ring bearing a monogrammed M. "What do you want to bet these are the keys to MaryMar's car? Well, that solves it. Lindsey, go find MaryMar and get her in here to take care of her friend."

"You better find a doctor, too," said Mam, who had turned her attention back to Lorna Spivey. "Her breathing's getting real shallow. Here, Bonnie, help me get her out of here and on the floor."

The thought that she might be going into respiratory arrest was enough to send me running out the door. Two steps up the sandy path, I almost collided with a short, elderly man in a white alligator golf shirt and windbreaker. Thanks to Mam, I knew he was the answer to our prayers—the urologist from Greenville.

"Good thing that doctor was right here," Bonnie said as we watched the EMS truck speed out of the gravel parking lot, red lights flashing in the dark. They hit the siren as soon as they got to the main road.

"It's lucky, too, the paramedics were using their dinner break to check out the Gatortorium," Mam said. She looked at her watch. "Amazing. That was one of the longest half-hours of my life. I hope Lorna's going to be okay. Oh, rats, I forgot to give them her purse when I turned over her wallet with her ID and all. Well, we can give it to MaryMar."

"If we can find her," I said.

As soon as I sent the doctor to help Mam and Bonnie, I'd found EMS and Turner Hickey, who discreetly directed some curious bystanders and latecomers toward the barbecue and away from the restrooms. "I think MaryMar's over there," he'd told me, frowning. "I got my snake from her awhile ago and wrote her a check. That red convertible in the parking lot's hers, so she must be around somewhere."

But after a quick scan of the crowd at the picnic tables, I'd trotted back. "No MaryMar," I'd reported, a bit breathless.

"She's bound to be around here," Mam told me now. "You just didn't look hard enough. You sure she's not in the reptile house?"

"No, Turner locked that when he took his snake in," I said. "He also locked Lizard Lodge—that's what he calls the office—though he had to let somebody in to use the restroom there, since these were tied up." I saw no need to tell them that someone was me. "And I did so look for her. I saw J. T. and everybody else down at the barbecue."

"Speaking of which, there better be some left," Bonnie said.

Between the snakes and Lorna, I wasn't hungry, but Bonnie was already leading us toward the picnic area like a hound dog on the trail of a coon—or in this case a hog. Mam went off to find J. T.

"Oh, that was good," Bonnie said ten minutes later, after polishing off a paper plate piled high with barbecue, beans, and coleslaw. "You get asked to a barbecue in D.C., and half the time it's just hamburgers, or maybe steaks. Those Yankees say *barbecue* when they mean *cookout* or *grill*." She poked a stray baked bean with her plastic fork. "I've given up telling people I'm from Indigo Island because they don't know anything about the Low Country except Charleston and Hilton Head and maybe Kiawah. And you want to talk about dumb blondes"—she gave her head a shake—"I had this woman at a deposition ask me, I kid you not, which one was on top, North Carolina or South Carolina."

"Geography must not be her strong suit," I said.

"That's the truth. And heaven help us, she works for the federal government."

"Let's hope it's not the post office," I said idly, drinking the last of my sweet tea.

"Still no MaryMar," Mam reported now, plopping down on the bench beside me. "J. T. says he hasn't seen her down here at all. He wasn't much interested in Lorna being drunk either. Everybody's talking about either basketball or that fancy boat Ron Simmons has got docked at the landing. Calls it the *Do Ron Ron*. I bet his wife just hates that. Course, I don't think she comes down here that much, even though they've got that big new house. Bonnie, you've got some barbecue sauce on your cheek. Lick to the left. What have I missed?"

"Zip," I said. "Or rather zip codes. Bonnie was lamenting that no one up her way has even heard of Indigo."

"Well, I think that's a good thing," Mam said. "There are too many new people as it is. I mean, tourists are okay, as long as they go back over the bridge at the end of the day, but it's getting so you can't find a parking place at the Pig on a Saturday."

The Pig was the Piggly Wiggly, the island's only grocery store. In the off-season, you could stop to chat with a neighbor or a cashier in the narrow aisles without fear of being slammed by a tourist wheeling a cart like it was a Humvee, intent on buying up every hamburger bun in the store.

"I know," Bonnie said. "I was just trying to figure out who a lot of these people are. Like, who's that talking to Posey?"

I looked at the group of men at a table down from us. Pinckney's groundskeeper's height gave him away. There was nothing small about Posey Smalls, who had once led the Granville Gators to the state basketball championship. "Lonnie Williams," I said. "He's the termite guy I told you about. And next to him is Mike Bishop. He used to be a yachtie, one of those private sailors who crews for rich people, lives on board all the time."

"I saw him with MaryMar earlier." Bonnie cocked her head to one side. "He's good looking, although I can't say I'm much for ponytails on guys. But he's got that Johnny Depp pirate thing going. You think he uses a conditioner?"

Mam ignored the question. "I wonder what he was talking to MaryMar about," she said. "I didn't know he knew her. He hasn't been here all that long. He's living down near the landing. He keeps an eye on a couple of boats, does some odd jobs, too. Allgood's uses him for big catering jobs, setting up, bartending."

"Okay," Bonnie said. "That's three out of four. Who's the white-rabbity one under the floodlight?"

"The wedding photographer. Mam knows more about him."

She nodded. "Lives in Charleston, name's Scott Russo. I think he must have allergies or something, which is why his nose is pink and twitchy. But you're right, he is kind of rabbity. Takes good pictures, though. He did some of the bridesmaids last week. Made them all look pretty, even the Gates girl, whose red hair just clashes something horrible with purple. He'll need to shoot MaryMar now." Mam stopped abruptly. She looked around to see if anyone was within hearing distance—they almost always were, in her case—then lowered her voice to a stage whisper. "What if MaryMar has been kidnapped? Did you ever think of that? Maybe somebody got Lorna drunk so they could get MaryMar out of the way."

"Mam, have you lost your ever-loving mind?" Bonnie put her cup down on the concrete table. "Good grief. Who would want to kidnap MaryMar? The next thing you'll tell me is that an escaped convict is hiding out in those bushes over there, or that Lorna was poisoned."

Mam's eyes widened. "Maybe she was. That's how it would be in a book or on TV. Something exciting."

I groaned. Bonnie raised her eyebrows and stared at her sister. Mam was a fan of *Law & Order*, having gotten hooked on the reruns. Since then, she'd discovered TV was rife with detective shows.

"Lindsey, why didn't you tell me it was this serious?" Bonnie said. "We may have to do an intervention." She looked across the table at Mam and intoned in her best lawyer voice, "Margaret Ann Matthews, you have been accused of *CSI* addiction. This is a serious offense against reality, and the penalty is me taking the remote away from you."

Mam had the good grace to grin. "Okay, okay. I'm just trying to liven things up a bit. This week's going to be pretty busy, with the wedding and all. Besides, there's nothing on TV I want to watch. It was sweeps last month, and now it's basketball tourneys. In fact, J. T.'s got some game he wants to see, so I guess we better go."

The party was breaking up. I looked for a platinum head, but there was still no sign of our missing actress. "Maybe MaryMar had a late date," I said.

"That would explain it," Bonnie said. "She came with Lorna and left with someone else, which would account for why Lorna had the car keys. I guess we better turn over this purse. Lorna's cell phone's in there, too, but before you ask, the battery's dead. Other than that, it's her makeup, Tic Tacs, and what looks like a hotel room key."

"You take it, Lindsey," Mam directed. "When you talk to Will tonight, you can tell him you have it."

"How do you know I'll be talking to Will?"

"Because you talk to him every night. Your line is always busy when I try to call. And now that you've got high-speed Internet, I know you're not on-line. Who else would you be talking to for hours on end?"

"I have other friends," I said stiffly. "And I talk to Mama. So there, Miss Smarty-Pants. And why would I talk to Will when I see him—"

"Gotcha!" Mam said triumphantly. "I told you, Bonnie. The girl's in love, even if she won't admit it. Come on, Lindsey, fess up. Is he a good kisser? Maybe you're not talking on the phone. Maybe you're unplugging the phone. Maybe—"

"Stop, stop," I pleaded. I was annoyed that I'd let myself be snookered by Mam. But her comment also reminded me that Will hadn't called last night from his conference. It was no big deal, but he was the one who'd wanted to rekindle the secret romance we had in college, when he broke my girlish heart. Mam and Bonnie didn't know about that, and I'd just as soon they didn't know about what was—or wasn't—going on now either. "I'm going home to walk my dog and cuddle my cat and go to bed with a good book," I told them. "Bonnie, I'll pick you up about ten to go to Centerville." Mam was leaving early in the morning for a flower pickup in Charleston, and I'd harangued Bonnie into going with me to Bayview to see Miss Augusta. "Really, Mam, you keep the purse. You can give it to Beth. She's the one who knows MaryMar and Lorna. I'm surprised you haven't called her already."

"I would have, but my cell phone couldn't get a signal. We're in a low spot."

That was no surprise. The entire island is a low spot. Cell phones work from the bridge, from the beach, from the second stories of some houses if you're sitting next to a window, and presumably from treetops. I'd once called Mam from the roof of my CR-V. I suggested that to her now.

"Don't be ridiculous, Lindsey," Mam said. "I'll just call her from home, although I must say I'm not looking forward to telling her one of the bridesmaids has gone missing. I hope she doesn't go to pieces on me."

"It won't be the first time," I said.

"Or the last," Bonnie chimed in. "Lindsey's right. MaryMar and Lorna aren't our problem." She nodded at Lorna's purse and smiled. "This time, Beth can be the one left holding the bag."

CHAPTER FOUR

Old South, New South

"What's in the bag?" Bonnie poked her nose in the brown Piggly Wiggly sack on the car seat.

"Oh, stick that in the back, would you? It's some stuff Miss Augusta wants. And there's nothing in there to eat, unless you count the Twinings tea."

"Why is it you think I'm obsessed with food?" Bonnie fastened her seatbelt as I backed out of Mam's drive, careful not to catch the pine tree on the curve with my side-view mirror. Really, that tree was a menace, which was why J. T. liked it—a natural speed barrier for the unwary.

"Because I know you," I told Bonnie, "and because our entire family is obsessed with food. It's genetic." I believed this with all my heart—and stomach. I also had proof. Other families had photo albums and home movies of kids learning to walk, teens dressed up for proms, parents with golf clubs or tennis rackets. We had page after page of what the cousins and I had dubbed "eating pictures"—snapshots of us crowding around loaded holiday tables, pound cakes and pies lining the buffet, my younger brother, Jack, waving a turkey leg the size of his forearm. Which reminded me of even more evidence. "You know how Jack has been researching the family genealogy?" Bonnie bobbed her head in acknowledgment. "So he's checking out the North Carolina Kinseys, and it turns out they're not Scots-Irish or English. Jack says they were with the Swiss Colony."

"The food catalog?"

"Ha!" I banged the steering wheel in triumph. "That's what I said. He meant the Swiss settlers who came over to New Bern. But when someone says 'Swiss Colony' and we automatically think about mail-order food, it says something about where our minds are."

"Swiss, huh? That could also explain our chocolate addiction."

"Exactly. We can't help ourselves. Mealtimes rule our day."

Indeed. Mam had called me during my breakfast of toast and Coca-Cola to report that Lorna was in intensive care at the hospital in Charleston, MaryMar was still AWOL, and Beth was taking the news as well as could be expected ("She didn't cry that much"). But Mam's main mission was to arrange where she would meet Bonnie and me for lunch in Centerville. The choices were limited to a few off-brand fast-food joints, an overpriced tearoom, a couple of pizza places, Allgood's Barbecue ("We had that last night"), and the China Palace, which was run by a good ol' boy who had married a Korean girl when he was in the army. We were leaning toward the tearoom in the bed-and-break-fast where MaryMar and Lorna were supposedly staying ("Maybe MaryMar will have turned up, and it has great chicken salad"). Then Mam suddenly remembered that she'd have fresh flowers in the van ("Those hydrangeas will need to go in water"). Unless Bonnie and I heard from her, she'd just meet us back at her house for supper.

"Bet you a buck Mam calls before noon and has figured out how to sandwich lunch in," I told Bonnie now, turning off the main road.

"I'm not taking that one," Bonnie said. "She'll call. Why are we going this way?"

"I need to stop and check the Finches' mail while they're out of town."

"And how is nosy Myrtle? I'd never let her check my mail. She'd probably steam open the envelopes."

"She's as nosy as ever," I said of our mothers' bridge-club president. "But I know you'll be pleased to hear her dear Dabney's diverticulitis has just about cleared up. Now, it's his allergies."

"Naturally. Oh, look at all those dogwoods. They just . . . For Pete's sake!" Bonnie whooped. "What in the world?"

"Finches' Folly. It's taken them forever to get it built. They just moved in a few weeks ago."

"It's a house? It looks like something from outer space."

"You've seen round houses before," I said, braking so Bonnie could fully appreciate what resembled a flying saucer—if you wanted the model with the gray wood paneling and red roof.

"But those houses are on the beach and have views. This looks like it crash-landed in the palmettos."

"Well, Dabney evidently goes for that Beam-me-up-Scotty thing. The paper ran a feature on him. His architecture office in Charleston looks like the space station, all chrome and modern."

"I wouldn't think that would go over real well with the locals," Bonnie said. "They want white columns and wrought iron—you know, either Charleston singles or their own taste of Tara."

"Most of Dabney's clients are out of state. He does right well."

"Is he delivering bread, too? Otherwise, why is there a bread truck parked there on the side?"

"Because he and Myrtle were living in their RV on the weekends while the house was being built. They didn't have enough room for everything they carted out here, so they used that old truck as an overflow closet. They call it the Carriage House."

Bonnie snickered as I pulled away from the mailbox. "If that doesn't about sum up the Old South colliding with the New, I don't know what does. Close encounters of the weirdest kind."

"This is weird," I said. "Have you noticed how there's no traffic coming toward us?"

We had bumped over the old drawbridge, which, if you were running late, was bound to be open so the big boats could navigate the cut on the waterway. We always added fifteen minutes to any trip off the island, just in case. Today, because we weren't in any particular hurry, we'd made the crossing with ease. Unlike the drawbridges that opened in the middle, the two sides poking up in the air, the middle section of our bridge slid to the side at an angle, creaking and groaning. Built during the Depression to replace an old barge ferry, it was now due for replacement itself with one of those high, arching concourses going up all across the Low Country. Islanders were of two minds about a new bridge. It would be nice not to sit on the wrong side of the waterway on a hot summer day worrying about your engine overheating or your kidneys giving out. But we also knew that the drawbridge, like J. T.'s pine tree, was a barrier. A new bridge would encourage more people to take the turnoff from the highway near Jacksonboro. If they went home at the end of the day, it was okay, like Mam said, but what if they wanted to stay? Developers already were circling the woods and tomato fields like vultures eyeing road kill.

"There should be some traffic, even on a weekday morning," I said. "The Pig gets deliveries, and there's the post office and UPS, plus people coming to Pinckney."

Miss Augusta was all for a new bridge. She was already planning billboards to bring in more tourists—or "guests," as she preferred to call them. "Guests, my eye," our great-aunt Cora sniffed, noting that "paying guest" was an oxymoron, like "jumbo shrimp." Aunt Cora opposed getting rid of the drawbridge.

I looked ahead at the two-lane blacktop slicing its way through the river basin, trees forming a lacy green canopy overhead. There wasn't a soul on the road but us. "I suppose there could be a tree down, or construction somewhere. I hope it's not a wreck."

"I'm sure Will would tell you."

I glanced at Bonnie, whose eyes were an innocent hazel. She didn't fool me one bit. She was just more subtle than Mam. I was the reporter in the family, even though I was just freelancing these days, but we all had our ways of weaseling news from people. Maybe if I didn't respond, she'd back off. She already knew Will was out of town, but here she was dangling the bait in front of me.

She leaned back in the seat. "Come on, cuz, give it up. I want to hear about you and Will. You know you want to tell. I remember how when I first started going with Tom, he was the only thing I wanted to talk about."

Ah, the full-frontal assault. I wasn't being hooked but netted. "Will helped me move my stuff from Charlotte." I didn't tell her the way our eyes had met over the old white iron bed in the front room as I'd piled it with several vintage quilts. Or how we burst out laughing when Will leaned across the bed to spread out the blue-and-white coverlet, only to discover that the large lump was Peaches the cat, who was not amused. "But between his schedule—he rotates shifts with the other deputies on the island, even though he's in charge down here—and me trying to keep Pinckney running, we don't see all that much of each other."

This was true, much to our mutual chagrin. Having lost almost twenty years between our brief college liaison and our recent revival after Will's divorce, we had plenty of catching up to do. And it was no help that when we did see each other, it was more often than not in public. We couldn't pretend to bump into each other on the beach or at the Beachside Café around noon. We were always running into someone we knew, many of them our relatives. Since Will's son, Jimmy, was dating Mam's daughter, Cissy, we had been at Mam and J. T.'s together a couple of weekend nights for supper, the guys grilling steaks or frying fish after messing about in the boat. But those evenings ended with Will and Jimmy heading home together and me going to Middle House to wait by the phone. Those sleepy late-night calls had become something of a ritual, and it bothered me that I hadn't heard from Will the last two days.

"But you want to see more of him, right?" Bonnie prodded. "I bet it's hard on the island, too, with everyone knowing everybody else's business. You never know who might be driving out by Middle House and see a patrol car or Will's truck."

Gee, she was getting too close for comfort. It was time to wriggle out of this conversation. "We've made such good time we can stop off at Sunset Court," I said. "Ray Simmons is turning it into this little shopping center. Each of the old tourist cabins is a small business. There's a place that does alterations, and Lucille moved the Cut 'n' Curl into what used to be the main building because it had the most room. The Sunset's right up the road here by the turnoff for the river road. We'll stop and see." I braked. "Or maybe we won't."

Flashing red and blue lights winked up ahead, competing with the sunlight bouncing off chrome. A red SUV that had passed us back before the bridge was last in a line of eight or ten cars and trucks stopped by a sheriff's cruiser and a barricade of orange traffic cones. People milled around open car doors, some talking on cell phones. I could see a fire truck, but all its hoses were in place, and a couple of firefighters were shrugging out of their protective gear. And why the Haz-Mat truck?

"Come on," I said, spotting the tall deputy we knew. "There's Olivia Washington. Let's go see what's going on."

Bits and pieces of conversation followed us up the asphalt.

"Let's reschedule for this afternoon."

". . . the darnedest thing."

"They say the road's going to open soon."

"It was a white van, I heard."

"That smell is awful."

"Phew! What's that?" Bonnie wrinkled her nose at the stench. "It's like, um . . ."

"Cat pee." Olivia grinned. "That, friends, is a genuine crystal meth lab, or what remains of it. You've missed most of the excitement. Lucille came in this morning and called us to say she thought something— maybe ammonia—was leaking from the janitorial supply business in the cabin down near the end. The first deputies here evacuated the place and called in Haz-Mat because they thought it might blow to kingdom come. But it's all cleaned up now. We're going to reopen the road as soon as they and the fire truck get out of here."

From where we were standing, I could see across the road to the

place the evacuees had gathered. Lucille fluttered around her early cus-
tomers in their floral plastic ponchos like a butterfly, pulling up a see-
through bonnet to examine an elderly woman's roots—that was going
to be some blue hair!—and whipping scissors out of her pocket to
straighten a little girl's wispy bangs. I ran my fingers through mine. I
hadn't had time to get a trim and had taken the fingernail scissors to
my bangs the other night. Lucille was going to have a fit.

"What is JS Company?" Bonnie asked. "It's on the sign next to the
Cut 'n' Curl."

"Janitorial supply," Olivia said. "We're trying to find the two men
who rented it, oh, just a week or so back. Lucille says they're hardly
ever there. She's only seen them early in the morning or when she was
closing up."

"Which makes sense if you're picking up cleaning stuff," I said.

"Or if you're covering for a meth lab." Olivia's walkie-talkie crack-
led from the loop on her belt, and she stepped away from us to listen.

"Redneck crack is what they've started calling it," I told Bonnie as
we watched the flurry of activity.

The fire truck had started its engine, as had the Haz-Mat truck,
which was beeping as it reversed. Bonnie gave it her lawyer look, no
doubt hoping that the locals knew how to clean up any spills that
might hurt the environment and spawn two-headed frogs or meth-ad-
dicted mosquitoes. The deputy up the road began collecting cones and
setting them on the grassy shoulder. People started back toward their
cars or toward the Sunset. Lucille's blue-hair hopped a cone before
Olivia could reach it. The notes of Pachelbel's Canon sounded faintly
from Bonnie's purse. I looked at my watch. It was getting on toward
eleven. Mam was early.

"What's that, Mam?" Bonnie put a hand to her other ear to block
out the noise. "You're breaking up. Let me call you back when we're in
the car, and we can talk about lunch before we go to Bayview." She
smirked at me, but then her smile abruptly vanished. "Okay, okay. We'll
be right there. I promise. Quick as we can. We're leaving right now."
She walked fast toward the CR-V, waving for me to follow. "Hurry,
Lindsey!"

"Why? Did she grab the last table at the tearoom?" I was practically running to catch up. "Are we going to meet her there?"

"No," Bonnie said. "The jail. She's been arrested!"

CHAPTER FIVE

Arresting Developments

"Okay, so I'm not really under arrest," Mam said, getting up from a padded chair in the reception area of the Granville County Law Enforcement Center. "But they said I have to stay here until they figure this out, so I might as well be."

"Hardly," I said. "You're not in a jail cell, for starters."

We were the only people in the small, carpeted area off the paneled hallway leading to the reception counter. Behind it, a deputy in Granville County khaki stood talking on a phone by a gray filing cabinet topped by a drooping plant. I could hear the crackle of police scanners, a familiar sound from my days as a reporter in Charlotte. Like all rookies, I had to take my turn covering night cops, which I thought was the worst of the crime beats until I covered weekend cops. There was a reason some guns were called Saturday-night specials.

"What in the world is going on?" Bonnie's voice was a mixture of relief and concern at not finding Mam behind bars on the other side of the building. "We're lucky Lindsey didn't get pulled for speeding. I tried to call you back but just got your voice mail."

"I was talking to one of my brides, who wanted to know how much more it would be to scatter rose petals not just down the aisle but when they leave the reception, too, or if she should stick to bubbles. I told her I'd have to get back to her, that I was tied up, so to speak." Mam, who'd been looking more put out than upset, suddenly started to tear up. "Oh, I'm so glad y'all are here. I just don't know what to do! It's all such a mess. J. T.'s not answering his cell, and meanwhile someone is ruining my good name!"

"There, there," Bonnie said, giving her sister a hug with one arm and taking Kleenex from me with the other. It was a good thing I'd thought to stash some in my purse after the Gatortorium to-do. "I'm sure we can work this out. Now, what's this about your name?"

Margaret Ann sniffed gratefully before continuing. "Some woman in Charleston is pretending she's me with a driver's license and a credit card."

"Identity theft," I said. "Are you sure?"

"I'm sure I'm Margaret Ann Matthews of Indigo Island. I'm not sure who this woman is who thinks she can sashay around the Low Country renting a truck in my name. They won't let me leave until the police in Charleston fax her picture, but the machine here's not working." Mam's voice still quivered but now with pent-up anger and frustration.

"Is that what happened?" Bonnie asked, frowning. "We need to cancel your credit cards right away."

"It's not my credit card she used. It's just a card in my name, which she stole before she stole the washing machine."

"Washing machine?" I asked. "I thought you said it was a truck."

"They were putting the washing machine in the truck."

"Who's *they*?" Bonnie sounded as confused as I felt. "You better start at the beginning."

The ensuing monologue was remarkably concise for Mam. She'd been driving from Charleston back to Centerville when a string of patrol cars with sirens blaring passed her. Then she'd come to a roadblock near the turnoff for the river road. A deputy had motioned her, another van, and a white truck to one side, after which she was asked for her license.

"Then he came back—he was just a baby, didn't look much older than Cissy—and he had Earl Crosby with him, and thank goodness, because Earl's known me since kindergarten, and he told me I needed to follow him back to the station because there was a problem with my license. I think if Earl hadn't been there, that other fellow would have put me in handcuffs and arrested me, and I probably would have called you from jail. But Earl said I was the real Margaret Ann Matthews and not this woman under arrest for stealing appliances out of a vacation rental house near Folly Beach." She stopped to take a breath. "So, if you look at it one way, I was arrested. Only it wasn't me. It's this other woman pretending to be me. I know I'm still me."

I nodded. " 'At least I know who I was when I got up this morning, but I think I must have been changed several times since then.' " Bonnie and Mam stared at me blankly. "*Alice in Wonderland,*" I said weakly. "You know, curiouser and curiouser."

"Curious is right." Bonnie sighed. "This is a fine hoop-de-do. But first thing, Mam, get out your credit cards, and let's call those toll-free numbers so they can flag them right away."

"All of them? Dillard's and Penney's, too? I haven't used them since Christmas. Just my Visa, I think. And J. T.'s."

"All of them," Bonnie said firmly. "Let's hope this woman didn't use them either. Maybe not, if she used a different card that has your name on it. But didn't the wholesaler tell you yours wouldn't go through yesterday? And this woman's got a driver's license with your name on it, and I'm thinking she may somehow have gotten your social-security number, too. You'd be surprised how many things it ends up on, stuff you carry around in your wallet. And once some thief gets it and a credit-card number, you can pretty much kiss your good credit good-bye. I bet neither one of you shreds."

Mam looked perplexed. "Sheds?"

"Shreds," Bonnie repeated. "Shreds. Like your old bills and applications for credit cards."

"Some people go dumpster diving," I volunteered. "They steal personal information and apply for credit cards in your name." I had a shredder, but it was in storage—along with all the stuff I'd never gotten around to feeding into it. Considering my pack-rat ways, I needed an industrial-sized one.

"Identity theft is the fastest-growing consumer fraud in the country," Bonnie said. "I know you've seen all those TV ads from banks. It can take years to straighten out."

"And I could have lived years without you telling me that, Bonnie Lynn Tyler!" Mam snapped. "I don't have years. I don't even have days, what with this wedding. And I've got a business to run."

"It won't take years," Bonnie said. "Sorry, I didn't mean to lecture. I can probably take care of most of it for you. We'll get in touch with the credit bureaus and get the forms. Here, give me your wallet, and we'll do the cards right now. And maybe Lindsey can find us a Coke machine."

"The break room's down the hall past the water fountain," Mam offered. I started that way but was brought up short by her shriek. "Water! Omigosh, the hydrangeas. I can't leave them in the van much longer in those boxes. I'm parked in the shade, but everything's going to start wilting if I don't get them somewhere cold fast. I can't believe I forgot about them. This is not like me. You'd think that woman stole my personality instead of just my name."

"No danger of that, sis," Bonnie said. "You are unique."

Mam grimaced and looked at her watch. "Does the jail have a cooler case? Aren't they always putting people in the cooler?"

"That's slang," I said. "There's probably a refrigerator somewhere, but you need something bigger."

"And colder, too."

"I've got an idea," Bonnie said. "Look out the window there and tell me what you see across the street."

"The dry cleaner's," I said. The sign in the plate-glass window announced an Easter special on dress shirts. "The feed store."

"No, next door to the cleaner's on the other side," Mam said. "Oh, Bonnie, you're brilliant. It's perfect."

I looked again. "I agree. Let's go check out the Easter specials at Pearcy's Fine Meats and Game."

"See, you two, there are advantages to living in a small town," said Margaret Ann, now back to being her usual in-control self. "It's real sweet of Hal to let us put the flowers in the meat locker."

"I think I'm going to become a vegetarian," I said. My previous experience with butchers was limited to the cellophane-wrapped steaks and ground chuck I bought at the Pig. Hal Pearcy not only supplied local restaurants and caterers with beef and pork, he also dealt with hunters who brought him deer, turkeys, and game birds. It had taken only one look at the open door of the locker, where the carcasses of large animals loomed from the shadows, before my Bambi complex set in. I'd retreated to the front of the store, but when I saw something labeled "tongue" in the deli case, I'd headed outside into the fresh spring air.

Mam and Bonnie had the back door of Mam's van open. Blue, pink, and purple blossoms were neatly lined up in plastic buckets. They looked in good shape to my untrained eye.

"If we do it like a fire brigade, it'll go really fast," Mam said. "Here, Bonnie, take these roses."

" 'Blue Curiosa,' " she read off the sticker on the plastic wrappers. "Even the flowers have curious names." She handed the bucket to Olivia, who we'd roped into helping us when she returned to the station. The desk sergeant had been reluctant to let Mam out of the building ("The fax repairman is on his way, but we can't let you go") until Olivia volunteered to keep an eye on her during her lunch hour.

"What's that song, 'Red Roses for a Blue Lady'?" Olivia had one foot on the sidewalk and one inside the door. "Mmm, mmm. Purple Veronica. Now, there's a name."

"Looks like Pinckney purple to me," I said.

I'd never seen so many different shades of purple. A sticker identified one bucket as Lisianthus, and I knew the flowering lavender stalks were Stock, which seemed a plain name for such a pretty flower. I scrambled into the back of the van for the Parrot tulips, only to be almost overcome by the heady scent of the pink Stargazer lilies behind them. Maybe they wouldn't smell so strong out in the air—or in the meat locker, where Hal, oblivious to the sweet stench of red meat, was placing the buckets. Mam was now working at a nearby sink and counter, filling containers with water for her precious hydrangeas, prepping them by cutting the stems with the small knife she always kept in her pocket for emergencies—like when she wanted a cutting from a Confederate rose, which wasn't really a rose at all.

But these last buckets were full of the real thing. " 'A rose by any other name,' " I muttered, backing out of the van on my knees. "Here, Bonnie, 'Hot Princess.' "

Bonnie tried to do a curtsy but tripped, grabbing the back door of the van so as not to land on her posterior. That she is such a klutz is why Mam and I are not insanely jealous of her head-turning good looks and fat-burning metabolism. It's a saving grace, so to speak.

"Oops!" she said with a grin. "Good thing Mam didn't see that."

"Didn't see what?" Mam said. She was standing in the doorway, her hand to her forehead as she looked into the sunlight. "Y'all stop fooling around or I'll put the law on you. Can't you keep these two in line, Olivia?"

Olivia sneezed.

"Bless you," we said automatically.

"Oh, excuse me," Olivia said, taking some Kleenex from her pocket. "Between the flowers and all this pollen, my nose has been itchy all day. Are we about finished here? I need to run by CVS and pick up my decongestant before I go back on duty."

"I just need the greenery," Mam said. "It can stay in the boxes, but it still needs to be in the cooler. Bonnie, look out! You're going to bend the Bells of Ireland! Those tops will snap right off if you're not careful."

⌒

"Vegetarian," Bonnie said, idly snapping a plastic coffee stirrer where she sat at the break-room table in the law-enforcement center. "I love tomatoes and butter beans and corn, but I can't imagine just living on them and salads. Still, I kinda know what you mean. That meat locker was right, uh, meaty."

"We should never have let Lindsey in there," Mam said. "Heavens,

43

she can hardly cut up a chicken, much less pluck a dove or a quail. I guess it's a good thing Will doesn't hunt." She eyed me. "Does he ever talk about it?"

"No, not really."

I knew she was talking about Will's father having been killed in a hunting accident when we were kids. His grief-stricken mother had gone back to work as a secretary at Granville High, and both Will and his older sister had worked after school and summers to help her make ends meet. Thanks to our high-school baseball coach, Will had gotten a scholarship to the University of North Carolina at Chapel Hill, where the coach's wife, my journalism teacher, also steered me. Will's sister was now a nurse in Columbia. Will had lived there, too, until after his divorce last fall, when he'd moved back to Indigo to the house where he'd grown up. His mother, a sweet-faced woman who sang in the Methodist church choir and kept a candy dish full of peppermints on her desk outside the principal's office, had retired several years ago to an apartment near her daughter's.

"She never really got over Dad," Will had told me once. "She hated it that I gave up on law school and became a deputy, carrying a gun."

I wasn't too keen on it either, though I was happy he'd rather fish than hunt. I was happy, too, that he cleaned his own catch. It wasn't that I didn't know how to fillet a flounder or, heaven help me, dehead shrimp, but I preferred that someone else do that part of the dinner prep. And since I hadn't lived on the island for almost twenty years until my return two months ago, I was also out of practice.

"It's too bad Will's not back. I'm sure he'd let me go," Mam sighed.

"I don't think he knows how to fix a fax machine," I said.

Yes, as Mam had pointed out, there were advantages to knowing everyone in a small town. But there weren't that many people to know. The one office-machine repairman worked out of his van and covered the whole county.

"But Will at least would let me go run some errands, instead of just sitting here. Of course, if Sheriff Floyd Griggs would get his big butt back from the VFW, he could sign off on me leaving." She stood. "I'm going to go see if there's any word yet."

Bonnie crumpled a yellow M&M's bag into her coffee cup. "Ladies' room?"

"Whatever." I followed her to the hall. I saw Mam standing by the counter and waved to her to let her know where we were.

"Another three stalls," Bonnie said, "but nicer than the Gatortorium."

"A little," I said. The tiled walls and floor were utilitarian gray. "It's clean, at any rate."

"And there's a hook for your pocketbook, and plenty of toilet paper."

"No drunks either." I squirted some pink soap on my hands and stuck them under the automatic faucet.

"Poor Lorna," Bonnie said. She was putting on lipstick, the same raspberry pink I'd admired the night before. "I bet she has a doozie of a hangover. She's gonna live to regret drinking that much."

Mam shoved open the door in time to hear Bonnie. "I don't think so," she said. "I just heard Lorna's dead!"

CHAPTER SIX

Lorna's History

"Dead?" Bonnie dropped her lipstick with a clatter on the Formica counter. I picked it up as it rolled toward the sink, then stared at Mam. She was leaning against the door to the bathroom so no one could come in.

"Dead," she said firmly. "I was standing there waiting when the call came in, and the dispatch person had her back to me and was repeating it while she wrote it down. 'Lorna Spivey dead. Need to notify emergency contact Mary Martha Futch. Autopsy scheduled for this afternoon. Call Dr. Markham A-SAP.' I wonder if whoever was on the other end really said 'A-SAP' or 'as soon as possible.' Not that it matters. Don't they only do autopsies when it's a suspicious death?"

"I don't know." I was still trying to process what Mam had said.

So was Bonnie. "What else did you hear?"

"Not much 'cause the scanner started crackling and another phone rang. I was afraid she'd turn around and see me, so I came in here real quick to tell y'all so we could figure out our next move."

"What next move?" Bonnie looked aghast. "Oh, no, you don't. You tell her, Lindsey. It isn't any of our business how that poor girl died. Maybe she had a heart condition. Let them find MaryMar. We are not getting involved in this suspicious death, or situation, or whatever you call it. Tom is going to stop me from coming home to Indigo if I keep getting involved with dead people. I want to spend the summer here, and maybe even buy some property for us to build on one day. But if you keep this up, Mam, my husband will think Indigo isn't safe for the boys."

"Pooh!" Mam pursed her lips. "That's ridiculous, considering you live in D.C." Bonnie started to say something, but Mam was on a roll. "You act like it's my fault Lorna went and died. I think we have an obligation after rescuing her from the Gatortorium to at least find out the circumstances. We're not getting involved. We already *are* involved. You tell her, Lindsey."

Oh, great. Now that they're grownups, the two sisters rarely argue, being of one mind on pretty much everything. Mam and I are more likely to butt heads, probably because we're so close in age and live near each other and are used to getting our own way. Bonnie's the peacemaker, although she can be opinionated and stubborn when she gets her dander up, like now. This was not going to be easy. The reporter in me agreed with Mam and wanted to know more about Lorna's death and MaryMar's whereabouts. But I also understood that if Will McLeod thought we were playing detective again, he'd have my hide. Then again, he wasn't the boss of me. And he wasn't even in town.

"I'll tell you what," I said. "Mam, since you have to wait here anyway, maybe you can offer to fix that plant of theirs that looks like it's about to keel over, or rearrange those dried flowers in the reception area. If you happen to overhear something else, fine, but don't go asking questions just yet. Maybe the subject will come up naturally."

Mam nodded happily. "I'm a good smoozer."

"Schmoozer," Bonnie said. "The word is schmoozer, as in schmoozing."

"Whatever. I'm good at it."

Bonnie appeared resigned. She knew that keeping Mam from

talking—about anything—was well nigh impossible. And Mam *is* good at schmoozing. We all are. We get it from our mamas, who've never met a stranger and can talk the hind leg off a donkey. Mam's just like them, only her donkey is legless.

"Meanwhile," I continued, "Bonnie and I will go and see Miss Augusta like we planned. I'm sure it's all over Bayview by now about the ambulance at the Gatortorium, and Miss Augusta will want all the details. And seeing how MaryMar was her protégé, Miss Augusta may know where she is. She may also know more about Lorna's history."

I handed Bonnie her lipstick. Mam was already out the door, mission unstoppable.

I spotted a familiar van as Bonnie and I crossed the parking lot. "I wonder if they know that Hired Killers are on the premises."

"Good grief! You told me he had a palmetto bug on top, but I didn't realize it was that size. I'm glad the boys haven't seen it."

It was indeed a nasty critter. "Nightmares?"

"Hardly." Bonnie shook her head. "No, they'd want one of their own to play with. Sam already thinks he's Spider-Man."

"Boys will be boys. Jack went through that phase, remember?" My brother was three months younger than Bonnie and had been the bane of our childhood, always pestering us to play GI Joe or superheroes. We were tomboy enough to like climbing trees and swinging on vines, but the older we got, the more girly we became, much to Jack's disgust. He figured Bonnie ending up with two boys was payback.

"Coca-Cola popsicles." Bonnie's voice was dreamy. We were both traveling down memory lane as we drove toward Bayview.

"Mam found some of those plastic molds at a garage sale," I told her. "We can make some popsicles this week if you want. We did when she first got 'em. But they weren't as good as I remembered."

"I know what you mean. One day last summer, I got a hankering for an ice-cream float, but I ended up drinking only half of it. But that was probably because Tom finished the vanilla and I had to use pistachio."

"Yuck. That would do it." I turned into Bayview's circular brick driveway. "And speaking of things not being like we remember, get a load of this place. This isn't your retirement home of yore."

"I'll say." Bonnie picked up a vase of mixed purple blooms that Mam had hastily assembled from the wedding flowers. "Very posh."

The two-story red-brick Georgian main building looked like a manor house, although a ramp on one side provided wheelchair access to the wide front door. Breezeways connected it to the long wings on either side. Azaleas flowered in landscaped beds beside giant oaks shadowing a green sweep of manicured lawn. Little Bay Creek, a winding branch of the Edisto River, meandered on the far west side of the grounds.

"Ladies." Mike Bishop, who was coming out as we entered, held open the heavy wooden door. "Those flowers are almost as pretty as y'all."

"Thank you, kind sir," I said. "I bet you say that to all the women."

Mike's easygoing charm fit him as well as the white shirt that emphasized his tan and the glossy darkness of his hair. "First ones today," he replied, his smile marred by a couple of dark teeth. Maybe dentists were in short supply on yachts. "Let me get you a cart from the front desk for that stuff and your flowers. I'd carry them for you, but I need to be over at Allgood's to make some more deliveries. We're behind because of that traffic tie-up this morning."

"Thanks, Mike," I said. "We've got it covered. Good to see you."

"You, too. Y'all take care, now."

Bonnie waited until I was wheeling the cart across the carpeted lobby. "If I was Will McLeod, I wouldn't go out of town and leave you in the vicinity of Mike Bishop. That is one good-looking guy, although he ought do something about those teeth. Still, I wouldn't kick him out of bed for eating crackers."

"Bonnie! And you a married woman!"

She laughed. "I didn't say I was inviting him into my boudoir." She deliberately drawled so it sounded like *boo-drawer.* "He wasn't looking at me anyway. Like I said, Will better watch out."

"Miss Augusta's *boo-drawer's* at the end of this hallway." I turned by a huge aquarium full of fish flashing gold and orange. "The administrative offices are upstairs. The elevator's over there, on the way to the dining hall and the activities room."

"It's like a really nice hotel," Bonnie said. "You'd never know it was assisted living except for these handicapped rails. It sure is quiet, though. Where is everybody?"

I looked at my watch. "Lunch is over. I expect people are either in their suites or playing bridge. Oh, and it's Tuesday, so there's bound to be a van over at Citadel Mall for the senior-citizen discounts at the department stores."

A calligraphy nameplate next to the closed corner door was inscribed with the name Townsend.

Bonnie knocked. "Miss Augusta," she called. "You've got company."

"More company," I said, hearing a murmur of voices inside.

Bonnie rapped harder.

"Come in." Miss Augusta's imperious tone made it seem more like an order than an invitation, but her smile was genuine when she saw it was us. I steered the cart into the living room, admiring the Aubusson rug from Miss Augusta's Charleston townhouse. She'd bought the townhouse after Colonel Carter Townsend's death more than twenty-five years ago, shortly before she began renovating Pinckney, and still used it as a second home. "Oh, I am popular today," she said from a wing chair by the window. "Maudie, look, the girls are here with some lovely flowers."

My elderly landlady was sitting in the twin of Miss Augusta's chair, her feet propped on a small stool. Her knee-highs peeped from beneath her floral print dress.

Bonnie leaned over to kiss Miss Maudie's pink, powdered cheek, setting the flowers on the pie-shaped table between the two ladies. Best friends since girlhood, the two octogenarians were a study in contrasts. Miss Maudie was as short and stout as the proverbial teapot and had curly white hair. Miss Augusta, taller and thinner to start with, had lost weight since she'd been sick, making her nose beakier than ever. With her rust-colored chignon, royal-blue quilted day gown, and embroidered Chinese slippers, she looked every inch the lady of the manor, especially as she used her silver-handled ebony cane to point at the bag I'd started to unpack.

"That can wait, Lindsey," she said. "You and Bonnie bring in those chairs from the bedroom and come sit a spell."

She waited until Bonnie and I were sitting on the needlepoint seats and until we'd exchanged pleasantries regarding everyone's health before getting down to business. "I was just telling Maudie about last night's unfortunate incident at the Gatortorium. One of the orderlies here said y'all found Lorna Spivey dead drunk in the ladies' room."

Dead drunk? Miss Augusta, who was looking expectantly at us, had no idea her figure of speech was all too apropos.

"Yes, ma'am, she appeared to have been drinking," Bonnie said. As she described the scene, both women leaned in to hear better. When Miss Maudie started fiddling with her hearing aid, Bonnie raised her voice even louder. This wing of Bayview would be able to skip the evening news.

"Well, I declare!" Miss Maudie tsked. "That poor girl has had a tragic life, bless her heart, but that's no excuse for such behavior. I just don't know what the world is coming to." She shook her head. "Of course, she has no people."

"Really?" Bonnie seemed as surprised as I was. We had so many people our family tree looked like an orchard. "Was she an orphan from the children's home?"

Miss Augusta sniffed. I immediately knew Lorna hadn't been in an orphanage. She once had people, only they weren't Miss Augusta's kind of people. Her words bore me out. "Her grandmother was that Mrs. Dunn who lived over near the train station and took in boarders. There was no Mr. Dunn."

"Now, Augusta," Miss Maudie said. "We don't know for certain she was a grass widow, though it's true it was just her and a daughter. That daughter was the first Lorna, although Mrs. Dunn called her 'Cookie' on account of her name being so close to those Lorna Doones everybody ate back then."

Miss Augusta sniffed again. She didn't have to say *tacky* for us to understand that one did not call one's children after baked goods.

"Cookie ran off in high school, maybe with one of the boarders. No one knows for sure, only that she came back a year or so later with a baby girl she called Little Lorna. Cookie lived with her mama and took over the boardinghouse when old Mrs. Dunn died, but then the train station closed, and I don't think there were many boarders. Cookie never seemed to lack for money, though. Augusta, do you need a hanky, dear? Lindsey, you can put the flowers up on the highboy. Now, where was I?"

"Cookie," Bonnie prompted. Having Miss Maudie relate "Little" Lorna's history was an unexpected bonus. Maybe because she watched so many soap operas—her "programs"—she had a storyteller's gift for melodrama.

"Yes, Cookie. To give her credit, she always made sure Little Lorna never did without. She sent her to dancing school, and she had piano lessons, too. But it was that baton twirling that she really took to. That was her talent in beauty pageants."

Miss Maudie paused. There was no need to recount the infamous evacuation of the Granville County Civic Center when one of Lorna's flaming batons ignited a small fire. Even people like Bonnie and me, who were living elsewhere at the time, had heard about it.

A sharp knock at the door interrupted our contemplation. A petite young woman wearing a pink uniform and carrying a chart stood in the doorway. "Mrs. Townsend, you're late for your physical therapy."

Sitting up straighter and fixing the pert woman with what we always called "the stare," Miss Augusta replied, "As you can plainly see, I am entertaining visitors and will not make therapy this afternoon. I will see you in the morning."

The little therapist started to say something but thought better of it and retreated, closing the door behind her. It was the signal for Miss Maudie to continue her story.

"Cookie, bless her heart, died not long after that. Pneumonia. She had weak lungs, always smoked like a chimney. Poor Lorna was left without any kin whatsoever, but she had the old boardinghouse. She sold it to the county, and that gave her enough money to go to cosmetology school up near Rock Hill. The next thing we heard, she'd married this no-account Spivey boy from somewhere in Tennessee. He'd just got out of prison for smuggling cigarettes, or maybe it was drugs, with a cousin. Still, he had a job as a mechanic, and everything might have worked out all right until the wreck. He was dead at the scene, and Lorna was in the hospital for weeks. That was when she got hooked on prescription painkillers."

Geez Louise, you couldn't make this stuff up if you tried.

"MaryMar came to her rescue," Miss Augusta put in. "She's always been a kind soul, and she helped get Lorna into one of those clinics like the Betty Ford. Then, when Lorna was rehabilitated, MaryMar had her come live with her and be her personal assistant. She does feet, you know."

"Feet?" Bonnie asked.

"Along with hair. And manicures, of course."

Oh, pedicures. But MaryMar a kind soul? My foot. She'd gushed all over me when she thought I was writing a magazine story on her, but as soon as she found out that I only wanted a quote about Watson the wonder dog, her expression had turned sulky. "He's a dog," she said. "He tried to eat one of my new Jimmy Choos. Look at the tooth marks on this heel. Oh, he's got everybody fooled into thinking he's so cute with that one-ear-up, one-ear-down thing. His owner says he was born that way, but I wouldn't be surprised if he had some work done." This from lips that owed their bee-stung beauty to collagen injections. But she smiled when I suggested taking a photo of her with Watson. "Oh, he's a sweet snookums puppy. Yes, he is." Watson had reacted with such comic confusion to MaryMar's baby talk that we'd used the resulting photo for the cover of *Perfect Pet*—minus MaryMar.

Bonnie's cell phone chimed Pachelbel from her purse. "Oh, excuse me," she said. "I thought I turned it off." She read the caller ID, snapped the phone shut, and stood. "Miss Augusta, Miss Maudie, I'm so sorry, but I need to go out in the hall and return this call. I won't be a jiffy."

"Oh, I hope it's nothing wrong, dear." Miss Maudie was all maternal concern.

"No, no," Bonnie said. "But if I don't call back now, they'll just keep calling."

It had to be Mam. I used Bonnie's absence as an opportunity to unpack Miss Augusta's belongings. She nodded approvingly at the small bedside lamp, the tin of Twinings tea, the framed miniature of her mother, a yellowing but unopened box of White Shoulders bath powder, and a copy of the latest Elizabeth Peters novel about Edwardian archaeologist Amelia Peabody. I could see where Miss Augusta would identify with the feisty Amelia. She probably had a pith helmet stashed in a closet at Pinckney.

"Oh, wonderful. I do so appreciate this." Miss Augusta frowned slightly as I unwrapped the china teapot from its bubble wrap. "Now, Lindsey, didn't Margaret Ann tell you I wanted the rose teapot from the attic?"

"Yes, but I couldn't find it right off, and this Wedgwood is so nice." I knew I should have braved the attic. "It's one of my favorites," I added hopefully.

Miss Augusta sighed.

"I'll take this one back and find the rose," I said quickly. "I know Beth is coming to Centerville tomorrow, and I'll send it by her." Maybe I could convince Posey to fetch it for me, or at least to accompany me up the narrow stairs to the third floor.

Bonnie came back in the room and signaled me with her eyebrows that we needed to leave.

Miss Maudie, who had nodded off in her chair, woke with a start. "Oh, do you have to rush off?" She reached into a Wal-Mart bag resting by the stool and pulled out a Whitman's Sampler imprinted with a Valentine's Day design. "Won't you have a piece of candy before you go? Augusta and I won't eat all this."

If Miss Augusta ate more than one piece, it would only be out of politeness. She knew as well as anyone that Miss Maudie had a backlog of Whitman's Samplers, thanks to her brood of gift-giving-challenged grandchildren. There was no telling if this box was just a month old or if the Valentine's wrapper was even from the twenty-first century.

I said as much, once we made our escape.

"She's a sweetie, though," Bonnie said. "But come on. I'll tell you

Mam's message when we get in the car, but the main thing is we have to pick up those dratted fish from GoodPet."

The clock by the front door said four forty-five. Where had the day gone? "We'll never make it back across town, this time of day," I said. "They close at five. Maybe Beth can pick them up tomorrow. I thought I'd send Miss Augusta's teapot by her."

"Give me that teapot. I have a better idea." Bonnie looked around the lobby. The receptionist had her head down, talking on the phone. "Here, stand in front of me so no one can see if they come in the door." She dunked the elegant Wedgwood teapot into the aquarium, scooping up several cups of water and one goldfish.

"We need two," I said, handing her the mini-net that was hanging on a nearby hook, no doubt so management could easily remove any belly-ups before residents spotted them. "I can't believe you're doing this."

"Neither can I, but desperate times call for desperate measures. Come here, little fella." A second fish plopped into the teapot, sloshing some water. "Oops. Let me wipe this up before some old geezer slips and breaks his neck."

"Or catches us. Hurry, here comes somebody."

A balding gentleman in suspenders held the door for Bonnie as she cradled the dripping teapot.

"Thank you so much for the cart," I said, returning it to the front desk. The receptionist looked up from the phone and nodded. It was a different woman than before, so maybe she wouldn't be able to pick us out of a lineup.

Bonnie was waiting for me to unlock our getaway vehicle. "All right!" she chortled as I pointed the CR-V toward the island. "Go, fish!"

CHAPTER SEVEN

This Can Only End in Tears

"It was like shooting fish in a barrel," Mam reported. "I took the plant into the ladies' room to give it some water, and while I was in there, I decided I might as well go. The dispatch girl came in, talking to some other woman about Lorna."

"They didn't know you were there?" Bonnie asked, handing me one of the plastic buckets of Purple Veronica.

We had arrived back on Indigo only a few minutes after Mam, and once we transferred the Bayview fish from the teapot to a tank in her den, we began helping her unload the van. The cooler in her garage was filling up with blossoms that seemed none the worse for having spent a few hours hanging out with hams and steaks. We understood from Mam's message on Bonnie's cell that she had stuff to tell us, but we knew none of the details. When we'd tried to call her back on the way home, we kept reaching the voice mail for Coming Up Roses.

"That was the amazing part," Mam said proudly. "I was in the far stall, and I just pulled my feet up. They didn't even see the plant on the counter. And I had my purse round my neck. I'm glad, though, that they had those sanitary seat covers."

"TMI," Bonnie said. "Too much information. What about Lorna?"

"They said they had to wait on toxicology reports from SLED, but meanwhile there was a BOLO out on MaryMar."

"In English, please." Bonnie was getting ready to treat Mam as a hostile witness.

"SLED's the State Law Enforcement Department," Mam replied. "They do the heavy-duty forensics."

"And BOLO is 'Be on the lookout for,' " I contributed. Mam wasn't the only mystery fan among us. Plus, I was dating a deputy. "They usually do it before an APB."

"All-points bulletin." Mam again.

"That one I know." Bonnie reached to get more buckets from me as I moved farther inside the van. "So what else? Was Lorna poisoned?"

"They're not sure, but one of the women started talking about how if you mix enough Xanax with alcohol, the person acts really drunk instead of poisoned. Evidently, there was a case upstate last year where a husband murdered his wife that way. At first, it was ruled a suicide, but then they found out he had a girlfriend and was hiding his assets."

"You heard all this in the ladies' room?" I was careful with the tender-headed Bells of Ireland on their tall stalks, remembering Mam's previous instructions.

"Yep. I might have missed some of it when they were washing their hands—like at first I thought they said *polo* instead of *BOLO*. And I was sure they'd see the plant, but they didn't. And then they left. I waited awhile before I came out, and by then Earl Crosby had found Sheriff Griggs and got him to sign off on me leaving. Earl made some calls to someone in Charleston, and the Margaret Ann Matthews they have in custody doesn't look anything like me. She has brown hair and blue eyes, but she's about twice my size." Mam spread her arms so she looked like a lady wrestler. "The real clincher, though, is she's a Yankee!"

"How could they tell?" Bonnie said as she helped me clamber out of the van and shut the back doors. "I mean, she has a South Carolina driver's license."

"Her accent." Mam laughed. "That was one of the things that tipped them off that she might not be me. As soon as she opened her mouth, she sounded more like Long Island than Indigo Island."

I turned on my headlights as I headed home, leaving Bonnie to fill Mam in on Lorna's history. Mam had asked me to stay for supper, but I was ready for an early night. I had to be at Pinckney first thing in the morning to find that rose teapot and get it to Beth. I did like the Wedgwood one better, but I'd never drink tea out of it again.

"Tell Cissy to come on home," Mam had said. "I know she was going to walk Doc for you after she left Pinckney, but it's about dark."

One of the conditions for Mam and J. T. finally breaking down and leasing a Honda Civic for Cissy was that she drive only during the day. As I pulled onto the oyster shells off the rutted dirt road, I saw the red Civic parked in the side yard, but there were no lights on inside the wide, white frame structure. That was odd.

"Cissy?" I called, walking toward the house. The huge pink azaleas that reached to the wraparound porch looked almost menacing in the deepening twilight, as did the silhouetted Spanish moss on the heavy oak limbs.

Something bounded out of the shadows.

"No, Doc, down." I fondled his yellow head as he butted against my waist, pawing me happily. "Yes, I'm home. No lick. Where's Cissy?" I knew she wouldn't let Doc out unless she saw me. He gamboled around me, plumed tail waving. I followed him up the wooden steps. Cissy was sitting in the porch swing, arms crossed in front of her chest. "Hey. What are you doing out here in the dark? Your mom said it's time for you to head home."

No answer.

"Cissy?" I opened the screen door and flicked on the porch light. She immediately put her arm in front of her eyes, but not before I spotted tear-stained cheeks. "Cissy, honey, what's wrong?"

Doc whined uncertainly, nosing Cissy's knees. She buried her face in his fur, her voice muffled.

"Come on, sweetie. What is it?"

She sat up. "You should have told me." Her voice was cold. "Why didn't you tell me?"

"Tell you what?"

"That Jimmy . . ." She faltered over the name, then regained control. "That Jimmy had another . . ." She hiccupped. "That Jimmy had another girlfriend." She dissolved into tears. I sat on the porch swing next to her, but she turned again toward the dog, who was wiggling between us, his toenails clicking on the worn planks. Her shoulders heaved. "You should have told me!"

"I didn't know."

She looked at me, her eyes red from crying. "You're not just saying that? Jimmy's dad never said anything to you?"

"No." Will had never mentioned that his son had another romantic interest besides Cissy. The two teens had been inseparable since last fall. "I had no idea." My tone must have convinced Cissy because she let me pull her over to my shoulder. Between Doc's licks and Cissy's tears, I was getting damp. "There, there. It'll be all right." My mind raced through the roster of their mutual friends, wondering what little hussy had gone behind Cissy's back.

"She's from off," Cissy said, sitting up. "I don't know her name. He knew her before he moved back to the island. He called me this afternoon from Columbia. Did you know he went up there to see his mama over spring break?"

I nodded. Will's ex-wife, Darlene, had remarried last summer. Her new husband was the state legislator she had an affair with when she was still with Will. We didn't talk about Darlene. She and Will were high-school sweethearts, and she'd been his hometown honey until his senior year at UNC. Then Will and I ran into each other one rainy day at the library. He'd broken up with Darlene over Christmas break without mentioning my name. Then, two months later, while I was waiting for him to return to Chapel Hill from what I thought was a road trip with his baseball team, Mam had called me from her dorm room at Columbia College. Knowing nothing of my relationship with Will, she'd excitedly reported the news. Will and Darlene had eloped.

Rumor had it Darlene was pregnant. "But those two have been together forever," she'd said. "We always knew they'd get married. This baby, if it's true, just hurried things up."

At least Jimmy—that baby—had the decency to call Cissy. Will had avoided me when he returned to campus—and for the next eighteen years. It wasn't until this past Christmas that I heard the full story. Or had I? That man was going to get a piece of my mind the next time I saw him.

"Oh, Cissy, honey, I'm so sorry." I thought of all the platitudes I could tell her. That Jimmy wasn't worth all those tears. That there were lots of other boys. That time would help, and things would work out for the best. But I also knew that none of it mattered right now. Cissy had been blithely sailing through her teenage years. Jimmy was her first serious relationship, and you never really recovered from that first love, that first betrayal. I remembered that gut-wrenching, kicked-in-the-stomach feeling. Poor Cissy.

She looked at me miserably. "What am I going to tell people?"

"That you decided to dump him," I said. "He was too possessive. You wanted to see other guys."

"But I just wanted him," she wailed.

I handed her the last of the Kleenex. "I bet Sue Beth and Wiley have some cute friends coming in for the wedding. You going out with a college boy will fix Jimmy's little red wagon."

"You think so?"

That Cissy would even consider the prospect of another boy's attentions made me think that perhaps her pride was hurting as much as her heart. "I know so. Come on inside now, and let's call your mom and tell her you're going to eat supper with me."

In the kitchen, I opened the freezer door and looked at the contents—peas and carrots.

Cissy took the bag from me. "Is this what we're having for dinner?"

"Nope. I want you to go in the living room and lie down on the sofa and put this on your eyes. It'll help get rid of the puffiness. Here, wrap the bag in a dishtowel. This way, by the time your mama gets here, she'll believe our cover story."

Cissy looked doubtfully at the bag but retreated with it to the living room.

I called Mam and explained the situation. Mam, of course, was torn between wanting to rush right over to console her only child and tracking down Jimmy so she could read him the riot act. "And to think of all the meals I fed that boy!" she exclaimed. "Does Will know about this?"

"He's never said anything," I replied truthfully. "But right now, Cissy is humiliated as much as anything. If you come here and fuss, she's not going to believe I told you that she's the one who decided to break up. She might even fall apart again."

Mam promised to let Cissy be. She said she and Bonnie would be over with some Ben & Jerry's after supper. "I've got Chocolate Chip Cookie Dough. That's her favorite. J. T.'ll be watching the basketball game. And this way, Bonnie can drive Cissy's car home. We'll have a mini chick night."

Doc chowed down on Purina while Peaches, my big orange cat, attacked the Science Diet that I spooned into his bowl. Let's see. What could I fix for dinner?

Ten minutes later, I carried a tray to the front of the house, both animals following me. "Cissy, put Peaches in my room and shut the door, please. Doc, you don't eat grilled cheese. Here, have a Breath Buster." I gave him the treat I'd put in my pocket. He trotted to the front door so he could eat it over the rug.

Despite saying she really wasn't hungry, Cissy ate most of her sandwich and fruit salad. "How do my eyes look?" she asked as we heard the sound of Mam's car.

"You look fine. Doc, stop barking. We have guests, not burglars. Chin up, Cissy. You answer the door, and I'll take these plates back to the kitchen." I scooped the damp towel off the coffee table. The peas and carrots could go back in the freezer for the next crisis.

I was pulling four spoons out of the drawer by the stove when Bonnie came through the swinging door from the butler's pantry. A twin door on the other side of the pantry opened into the spacious dining room, where French doors on the opposite wall led to the living room. The layout was almost identical to the house in which our widowed grandmother had raised her three girls. We'd spent many hours there as kids and still mourned its loss shortly after Nanny's death, when a tropical storm felled an ancient oak that crushed one side.

"The support beams are gone," Uncle James, an architect, had said, surveying the damage. "The dirt's worth more than trying to rebuild. Just be thankful it was empty and no one was hurt."

But we still missed it, and the chance to live in Middle House had been one of the factors that helped me decide to move back to the island. Bonnie looked appreciatively around the kitchen now, taking in the old oak table, the single light bulb hanging over its center, and the humming Frigidaire that was almost as old as she was.

"Nanny had linoleum," she said. "Otherwise, it's almost just like her kitchen."

She gave a small sigh, and I thought, not for the first time, how our longing for Coca-Cola popsicle molds, Fireking dishes, and other vintage items was an attempt to recapture our past, when life had seemed a lot less complicated. We'd been as green as a spring day when we sat in the dogwood's sturdy branches or lolled on cots on the back sleeping porch reading Nancy Drew and Judy Blume while rain tattooed the tin roof.

"You could do a lot with this place," Bonnie said. "It has good bones."

"But it's not mine," I reminded her. "And it needs a lot of work, like a new roof."

"And central heating." Bonnie shivered. The temperature had dropped with the sun. "Maybe I don't want any ice cream."

I looked at her in astonishment. "Who are you kidding? You just don't want to light the gas heater in the living room. Here are the matches. Get Mam to do it. It scares me, too."

"Do you ever get scared out here in the dark all by yourself?" Cissy put her empty ice-cream dish on the tray and walked over to stare out the front window.

"I'm hardly by myself," I said, gesturing at the dog, who was doing his road-kill imitation, asleep flat on his back, paws in the air. "Doc's better than a burglar alarm." Doc flicked his ears at the sound of his name and half-opened one eye. "He's more likely to lick someone to death than bite them, but he sounds like he'd tear your throat out."

"Maybe we need him at Pinckney."

"Why?" Mam's loaded spoon was halfway to her mouth, but Cissy's words had her on mother-hen alert. "Did you hear something? I thought the ghost has been pretty quiet lately."

Bonnie and I exchanged looks. Whether or not Pinckney was haunted was an ongoing topic of local debate, as was the identity of any possible phantom. Mam was sure it was a crazy relative of the Pinckneys who'd been locked in the wire cage in the attic in the days before the hollerin' house—as we referred to the state mental institute—was built off the Savannah highway. That Miss Augusta wouldn't discuss the subject or let us mention it in the script for the tour guides was all the proof Mam needed. A resident ghost, after all, was nothing to be ashamed of. Indeed, it was a status symbol and a draw for tourists, who loved stories of secret doors, odd noises, and shape-shifting shadows. If the ghost was that of a plantation belle whose star-crossed love for a Union soldier had led to her untimely death—as one legend had it—Mam was sure Miss Augusta would acknowledge, even exploit, the restless spirit.

"No, this wasn't the ghost," Cissy said matter-of-factly. "It was somebody or something outside the back parlor windows after we closed today."

"Posey," Mam said.

"No, he'd already left to carry Marietta home," Cissy said. "There weren't any cars in the visitor lot either."

This was worrisome. "I'll call the security guy tomorrow and talk to Posey," I said. "It might have been someone on the landscape crew working late. Or maybe it was an animal. Most don't come out till night, but did you know we've got armadillos now in the Low Country? They've migrated up from Florida."

"Considering how most of them get run over, it's a miracle they made it as far as Georgia," Bonnie said, wrinkling her nose. "Possums in armor."

Doc's sudden growl startled us all. In an instant, he'd gone from playing possum to alert guard dog. Standing up, ears pricked, he looked more like a German shepherd than a Lab-golden retriever mix. My vet speculated that his heritage also included Russian wolfhound. There were no wolves on Indigo, but bobcats still prowled the deep woods of the island's interior.

"What is it, boy?" I asked as he joined Cissy at the window, still growling. The fur on his back was raised. "Cissy, turn on that lamp, will you?"

We all jumped when the bulb popped. There was still light from the flickering blue glow of the gas heater and the table lamp next to the couch, but the night outside had grown darker and the shadows inside deeper while we talked.

A spoon dropped into an empty dish made us jump again.

"Geez, Mam," Bonnie said. "Watch out. You woke up Peaches." But the cat, who'd been released from the bedroom to sleep on a cushioned window seat, was staring outside, his tail twitching. "Do you see something, Cissy?"

She cupped her hands around her face, peering out, then drew back suddenly. "Y'all come here, quick! I swear I'm not making this up, but there's something white out there. It looks like a ghost!"

We jostled for position around Cissy. Doc's growls turned into sharp barks.

"I don't see anything," Bonnie said.

All I could see was her head. I stood on my tiptoes, trying for a view over her shoulder.

"I think I do." As usual, Mam was front-row center. "It's white and flickering. See, over there?"

I still couldn't see around them. I crouched next to Doc and tried to wedge in.

"Maybe it's foxfire." Bonnie sounded doubtful. "You know, swamp gas?"

"We're nowhere close to the swamp." This was useless. I stood and headed toward the windowed door in the front hall.

"There. See it?" Mam again. "Whatever it is, it's getting closer. It's coming up the driveway. But I don't think it's a ghost. It's someone walking up the driveway in a white coat and hat."

"I see them, too!" Cissy yipped.

I grabbed Doc's collar and reached for the front-door knob. The only way I was ever going to see anything was if I opened it. Bonnie crowded behind me in the entrance hall, picking up the coconut off the table, a souvenir of Miss Maudie's long-ago honeymoon in Florida. "You've got the dog," she said defensively. "This is backup."

Cool air streamed in. Doc strained against my grip, nose nudging the screen door. The porch light reached only as far as the steps, but now I could see the figure coming closer. No ghost. And no hat either, just platinum-blond hair.

"For Pete's sake," I said. "It's MaryMar."

Chapter Eight

Caught in the Middle

"MaryMar!"

Mam's shriek in my ear was enough to stop the missing brides-maid dead in her tracks.

"Did somebody call me?" The voice wafted out of the darkness. "Is that you, Miz Frampton? I can't hear over that dog barking."

"Hush, Doc. It's a friend." That was stretching it a bit, but *acquaintance* wasn't in his vocabulary. He quieted as I stepped out on the porch, but I kept a tight hold on his collar. "Hey, MaryMar," I said. "It's Lindsey Fox and my cousins. I'm renting from Miss Maudie. The dog just needs to be introduced."

"All right, then." She moved into the light. What Mam had thought was a white coat was actually a terry-cloth bathrobe, the long, fluffy kind you find in spas and expensive hotels. What was either a small tote bag or a large purse was slung over one shoulder. "I was hoping I could use your phone. I can't get a cell signal out here."

"Sure, come right in." Mam had taken over as hostess. "My goodness, we thought you were a ghost walking up the drive. What brings you out here? Did your car break down?" Mam had apparently forgotten that MaryMar's convertible was in the Gatortorium parking lot or, more likely by now, police custody.

"Um, no, not exactly." MaryMar stood stiffly as Doc checked her out. "Okay, dog, that's enough sniffing. Can't you put him up?"

"It's his house," I said. "He won't bother you now. Cissy, would you please take him in the kitchen and give him a treat?" Cissy didn't want to be left out, but her mother's shooing motion and frown sent her on her way. "MaryMar, I'm not sure if you remember Margaret Ann's sister, Bonnie Tyler. Bonnie, this is Mary Martha Futch. She's going to be in Sue Beth's wedding."

MaryMar cringed at the sound of her full name. "I go by MaryMar." Her thick-lashed blue eyes quickly sized Bonnie up as possible competition, until she saw the gold band and diamond. Still, the subsequent smile didn't reach her eyes. "It's nice to meet you. I think I remember you, but I was just a little thing, and you must have been in high school."

"Middle school," Bonnie said, having taken MaryMar's measure. "May I take your, uh, coat?"

"Thank you." MaryMar shrugged out of the bathrobe as if it were sable, revealing a clingy white blouse that tied at the waist of denim capris. The white sandals were identical to Lorna's, but MaryMar's toenails were seashell pink. She must have thought we were all staring at the robe. "I wasn't expecting it to be so chilly. I was supposed to meet a friend this afternoon, but we must have crossed signals." She paused. "The phone?"

"Right here."

MaryMar took the portable from me and looked at us. Evidently, she expected us to leave the room.

"Why don't you go in here so you can have some privacy?" Bonnie's voice was all honey and syrup as she ushered MaryMar into the front bedroom and quietly closed the door. She put her finger to her lips and motioned us into the dining room. "So that's MaryMar. What a piece of work!"

"Did you see that outfit? It's just like Lorna's." Mam flushed with excitement. "She looks better in it, of course. I'd forgotten how much she looks like Marilyn Monroe."

"More like Madonna trying to look like Marilyn," Bonnie said. "She's more cat than kitten."

No wonder Beth was worried about MaryMar upstaging the bride.

"I wonder where she's been?" Mam couldn't stand still. She's a fidgeter even when she's supposedly relaxing. She can't watch TV without doing something with flowers or running up a hem. She twists her hair while reading a book or talking on the phone. Now, she was straightening the place mats on the dining-room table. Maybe if I handed her the Pledge, she'd polish the chairs.

"I want to know who she's calling." Bonnie sank into the recliner by the French doors. "She can't possibly know about Lorna, or that the sheriff's looking for her. We probably ought to call and tell them she's here."

"Not till she gets off the phone." I looked at the closed door. I didn't like MaryMar being in my bedroom, eyeing the T-shirt I slept in draped over the end of the bed and the jumble of stuff on the nightstand. She looked like a snooper, someone who'd peer in drawers and open the medicine cabinet in the bathroom. "What should we tell MaryMar about Lorna?"

Bonnie and Mam were saved from answering when MaryMar came out of my room. She seemed put out. "When a cell phone just keeps ringing, doesn't it mean the battery's dead? Because if it's just cut off, I always get voice mail. Or maybe it's not getting the signal."

I started to say something, but Mam cut in. "Don't you have a land-line number?"

MaryMar's forehead creased slightly. "I might could try the bed-and-breakfast in Centerville. Do you have a phone book?"

So she probably was trying to reach Lorna. Mam looked at me. I looked at Bonnie. Bonnie looked at MaryMar. "Um, MaryMar," she started, but was immediately interrupted by the sound of a car coming up the driveway. Doc, barking his head off, bounded to the door with Cissy in hot pursuit. I reached for his leash on the coat tree and snapped it on his collar. Now might be a good time for Cissy to take him for a walk.

"Evening, Margaret Ann."

Just the sound of Will's voice made my heart do a little flip. As for the sight of him, he looked as good in his sheriff's uniform as he had back in his baseball pinstripes in college. The years had been kind. Gray sprinkled the thick, dark hair at his temples, and little crinkles made his blue eyes seem even narrower above his clean-cut features. He'd filled out some in the chest and shoulders. He was lean now rather than lanky, a man instead of a boy. But the Will I had loved and lost back then was still very much in evidence. He said I hadn't changed either, except for my hair, which was shoulder length now instead of halfway down my back. Mirrors don't lie, though. Sure, I'm still waiting on cheekbones—and probably will till the day I die—and my nose will always turn up, making me look younger. But sunscreen and moisturizer have become daily necessities, and I keep trying to lose the five extra pounds that have settled on my hips.

We see what we want to see, I guess. I couldn't look at Will—or Mam or Bonnie, for that matter—without also seeing their former selves. When Mam laughed, her mouth wide, she was again my six-year-old partner in crime, plotting an escapade from the porch swing. All Bonnie had to do was knot her hair on top of her head to remind me of the Sunbeam Bread girl. And when Will's knowing eyes reached across the room and found me, like now, the years fell away, and I was the girl in the college library who found love on a rainy day in a familiar face from home.

"What are you doing out here, Will? Is this an official call? Are you on duty?" Mam's peppering hardly gave him time to answer.

"There's a report of a break-in at the Simmons home. Ron's wife, Elise, drove over from Charleston this evening and said someone had been in the house. I thought I'd stop here on my way back and make sure everything's all right." He reached down to pet my adoring dog, who couldn't decide which was better, attention from one of his favorite people or an unexpected nighttime walk. Will made up his mind for him, holding the door open. "Hey, Cissy. Look out he doesn't pull you down those stairs."

She nodded before ducking into the darkness, flashlight in one hand. If Will was surprised by the coolness of her response—she was usually as chatty as Mam—he was even more surprised to see MaryMar, her pale blond hair backlit into a halo by the light from the dining room.

"Hello, officer," she said. There was a slight huskiness in her voice I hadn't heard before. "I don't believe we've had the pleasure. My friends all call me MaryMar. I just came by to use the phone."

"Only she didn't get an answer," Mam put in. "Do you need a glass of water, MaryMar? You sound like you've got a frog in your throat."

Bonnie's attempt to stifle a giggle ended in a cough. "Excuse me." She used a tissue from her pocket to hide her face.

My turn. "Major McLeod, this is Mary Martha Futch." Will's reaction to the name was almost as imperceptible as MaryMar's shoulder twitching. "She's originally from Indigo and was at the Gatortorium opening last night. We missed seeing her, though. Didn't you leave early?"

"Not that early," MaryMar said. "I was meeting a friend."

"The same one you tried to call just now?" Mam was polite, but I could see her gearing up for a cross-examination. And to think it was Bonnie who was the lawyer.

"No, I was trying to reach my personal assistant. She has my car and was supposed to pick me up this afternoon." The seductive voice now had a hint of petulance. "It's not like her to let her cell-phone battery die. She's such a control freak, always tapping things into her Palm Pilot. She keeps track of all my appointments. Really, it's very selfish of her not to be in touch."

"Miss Fox," Will said, looking at me. He had caught the cue I tossed him. "Perhaps I could talk to Miss Futch—MaryMar—in your front room. Maybe I can help her."

I just bet he could. "It's that door over there." Like he didn't know.

"Oh, that would be so kind of you." MaryMar was smiling. "Are you sure we haven't met somewhere before?"

Ye gods. Did she memorize old movies?

"I'm sure I would have remembered." Will winked at me as he closed the bedroom door.

"Since when did Will start calling you Miss Fox?" Mam asked.

"Since he's obviously on duty." I wondered when he'd arrived back on Indigo.

"My guess is he's going to tell her about Lorna," Bonnie said. "Poor Lorna. MaryMar doesn't sound like much of a friend."

"I want to know what they're saying." Mam gazed at the door in frustration. "That thing where you hold the glass to the wall doesn't really work. Remember, we tried that at Nanny's when we got sent out of the room because she wanted to talk to Aunt Cora about somebody's womb or ovaries and didn't think we were old enough to hear."

That gave me an idea. "Shh." I lowered my voice. "We have to be really, really quiet."

"Y'all stop looking at me like that," Mam said in one of her stage whispers that can reach the back row. "I know how to be quiet."

"Not a word or a whisper," Bonnie said.

I used the remote to turn on the TV. "Did you see that pick-and-roll?" said the announcer calling the basketball game.

"I thought you said for us to be quiet." Mam struggled mightily to whisper.

"Will is bound to know something's strange if he doesn't hear any sounds," I said. "Now, follow me."

I tiptoed down the hall to the middle bedroom and opened the door. It gave a small shudder, but there wasn't enough noise to alert Will and MaryMar. Now, if the closet door on the left wouldn't squeak. . . .

Bonnie and Mam caught on immediately. Just like in Nanny's house, this closet backed up to the one in the front bedroom. But where there had been a thin panel separating the two at Nanny's, this closet was divided only by a metal bar, on which hung a clothes bag and a couple of bulky coats. I kept the closet door in the front bedroom cracked because Peaches loved to sleep in the laundry basket nestled among my shoes.

The old-fashioned doorknob turned easily under my hand.

"Now, Miss Futch—MaryMar—let me see if I have this straight." Will sounded like he was standing in the room with us, which he practically was. "You haven't seen or heard from Lorna Spivey since you left the Gatortorium last night?"

"No, I told you I haven't," MaryMar said. "It was all set up for her to take my car to Centerville and then come get me this afternoon. But she didn't show up, and then I fell asleep, and it wasn't until I woke up that I started getting worried and trying to call her."

"Where were you?"

"I'd rather not say." MaryMar sounded coy. Mam, who was kneeling between me and Bonnie, poked her head between the coats in front of us, parting them so we could see a small slice of the front room. She reached out to move the boots that partly blocked our view, but Bonnie grabbed her arm. A faint smell of mothballs emanated from the quilted plastic clothes bag next to me. "Oh, all right." A creak told me MaryMar had sat on my bed. I could just imagine her gazing up at Will. "If you must know, I was at Ron Simmons' house down the road. I star in his commercials."

"And were Mr. and Mrs. Simmons with you?" There was silence from the front room, but I could hear Mam's indrawn breath. "Miss Futch?"

"Mr. Simmons, okay? But he left around two for a business appointment in Walterboro." Mam let out her breath in a gasp. I tensed, sure that Will had heard it. "I don't see what my being with Ron has to do with Lorna," MaryMar said. "Shouldn't you be trying to call someone and find her?"

"I'm very sorry to tell you this, but Lorna Spivey was taken to the hospital last night. She died this afternoon."

"Died? Lorna died? That's impossible. She isn't sick." The bed creaked again as MaryMar stood. "What happened to her?"

This should be interesting.

"She collapsed last night at the Gatortorium. Can you tell me, did she have any problems with drugs or alcohol?"

"She didn't take drugs. Well, not anymore, not since she got out of rehab last year because of that painkiller thing. She hated to take even a Tylenol if she had a headache. She had a couple of drinks now and then when we'd go out somewhere, or a glass of wine. It was okay because I'm always the designated driver. I don't drink because of my anxiety medicine. I'm very high strung." Ow. Mam's elbow caught me in the ribs. "I think I better lie down. This is all such a shock to me." My bedsprings again. And no doubt my pillowcases. I'd just changed the sheets this morning.

Mam couldn't stand it. She edged forward on her knees, reaching out her arm to ease the door wider. Bonnie tried to stop her, but it was too late. The door swung wide at Mam's touch, even as she collapsed on top of my old tennis shoes. Bonnie fell on top of her. I wriggled back behind the clothes bag.

"Hi, Will. We were just looking for something in the middle-room closet." Mam gave it her best shot. "Did you know there's no wall here? I was so surprised. I just fell right through the coats."

"I can see that." Will's tone was neutral. "Why don't you and your sister get up and join us?" I held my breath. Maybe he hadn't seen me. "Miss Fox, too."

Rats. I crawled out after Bonnie, dragging a couple of fallen coat hangers with me. Will extended his arm to help me up. His grip was like a vise.

Mam unabashedly turned her attention to MaryMar. "Oh, we are so sorry about Lorna. We didn't know how to tell you that she was dead. See, we were the ones that found her last night at the Gatortorium, passed out in the ladies' room. You know, at first we thought she was you because of her hair and clothes. And we thought she was drunk because we didn't know then that Xanax and alcohol can kill you." Mam stopped abruptly, realizing she'd said too much.

"You three . . ." Will's voice was icy. "I'll deal with you later."

"You thought Lorna was me?" MaryMar sat up straight. "Oh, no. No, it can't be. He doesn't know I'm here. There's no way. It's impossible." Her voice was rising.

"Who?" Will turned from the three of us. "Ron Simmons?"

"No, no." MaryMar shook her head. "Not Ron. This guy. He's a stalker. He's been following me, sending me letters."

"You're being stalked?"

"That's why I came to Indigo, to get away from him. Really, you have to believe me. I have the letters in the trunk of my car. Lorna put them all in a folder." MaryMar's eyes widened. "Omigod! Don't you see? He's after me. He killed Lorna. He thought she was me! You have to protect me! He's here!"

As if on cue, the front door opened, the screen door slamming. We all jumped at Cissy and Doc's return. Except for MaryMar. She fainted.

Chapter Nine

Beds and Breakfast

"I'm still not sure that was a real faint." Bonnie poured herself another cup of coffee and sat down at the kitchen table at Pinckney. "She's such a drama queen that it's hard to tell."

"She woke up quick enough when Cissy put that frozen bag of peas and carrots on her face," Mam said. "Did you teach her that, Lindsey? I like squash better because you don't get those peas poking you in the eye like rocks. Remind me and I'll give you some I put up at the end of last summer."

"To eat, or for a cold compress?" I could use the latter about now. Too little sleep had given me a dull headache. When I'd arrived at Pinckney this morning, the cousins were already in the kitchen with Marietta. But they waited until she went to check on the cleaning crew before starting in on the previous night's events.

Will had told us that if we breathed a word, he'd lock us all up.

"You wouldn't," Mam had said.

"Oh, wouldn't I? I believe that you're wanted for robbery in Charleston."

"That's a mix-up, Will McLeod, and you know it! I'm the vic in that case."

"The vic? Margaret Ann, you watch way too much television." Will ran his fingers through his hair in exasperation. "The three of you think this is all a game. As for victims, there's a dead woman in the hospital morgue and another lying in there on Lindsey's bed who claims she's being stalked, but they are cases for the proper authorities. Bonnie, you're a lawyer. Would you like to explain to these other two the penalties for impeding a criminal investigation?"

Cissy's entrance from the kitchen with a glass of water for MaryMar interrupted his lecture. She glared at Will before going into the front bedroom to practice her candy-striping skills.

"Now, what have I done to her?" He seemed genuinely bewildered.

"Your two-timing son," Mam said, remembering she had another reason to be mad at Will.

"Jimmy?"

"You have only one son we know of, and he just happened to re-member when he called Cissy from Columbia that he has another girl-friend." Mam crossed her arms.

"It's a good thing Cissy was already dumping him." Bonnie struck the same pose.

"She was?"

"You bet," I told Will, crossing my arms, too. "She wants to date other guys."

"So what difference does it make if Jimmy's seeing someone else?" Looking at us lined up like the Three Musketeers, Will quickly real-ized his mistake. "But let's stay on the subject here, which is letting me do my job without your interference. Until I verify MaryMar's story, I don't want anybody knowing you've seen her. Margaret Ann, I'm count-ing on you to impress this on Cissy. Not a word to anyone, even J. T."

Mam looked mutinous. "But I tell J. T. everything! Well, almost. I didn't tell him about Lorna dying, but that's because there hasn't been a chance."

"And let's keep it that way. Bonnie? Lindsey?"

Will's tone brooked no argument. Bonnie and I both nodded. Before Mam could put in two more cents—or several dollars—about Lorna and MaryMar, Will ushered the sisters and the still-baleful Cissy out of the house.

When my phone rang ten minutes later, Will had picked it up before I could answer and told Margaret Ann there wasn't anything she had to tell me that couldn't wait until the next morning.

Now it was the next morning, and Mam said, "I was only going to tell him that it was just common courtesy to let Beth know that her missing bridesmaid had turned up, and that MaryMar probably could double up with Sue Beth if Will didn't want to carry her back to the bed-and-breakfast in Centerville. I know she'd already checked in and her clothes were there and all, but it seemed silly for her to go back last night when anybody and his brother could see her."

I listened to her prattle on as I took a long swallow of Coca-Cola and waited for the caffeine to kick in. Bonnie practically goes into Starbucks withdrawal when she's on Indigo, but I've never developed a taste for coffee. Neither has Mam, who drinks orange juice by the gallon and whose body seems to naturally produce some caffeine substitute. A glass of iced tea for lunch wires her until bedtime.

"Give Will some credit," I said, rattling the ice in my glass. "He wants her kept out of sight."

"You mean MaryMar's not in Centerville at the B&B?" Mam asked. "Well, where is she, then? I know Will said not to talk about her, but I'm sure he didn't mean us."

Bonnie grinned. "I'm sure he did, dear sister. But he also thinks Lindsey won't say anything. Obviously, he doesn't know she has ways of imparting information when need be."

"When need be." My smile was conspiratorial. Bonnie knew how this worked. I just had to be careful how I chose my words. "I think it would be a good idea if maybe y'all happened to drop by Middle House at lunch with a tape measure. I'm thinking about rearranging some furniture, and I need your help figuring out where to put the bed."

"What has your bed got to do with MaryMar?" Mam said. "You

mean she's at Middle House? In your bed? Land's sake, why didn't you put her in one of the other bedrooms?"

"Because it was easier than lighting another heater and making up another bed," I said, dropping all pretense, now that they had it figured out. "Or dealing with MaryMar, for that matter. What a diva!"

A diva with no sense of humor. She'd been none too happy about being stashed with me. Neither was I thrilled about it, but it made sense, especially in light of the alternatives, like Will driving her to some safe-house motel on the Savannah highway or, heaven forbid, taking her home with him. She'd suggested as much.

"That way, I know I'd be safe," she'd said, looking up at him through downcast lashes. "Because you'd be there."

"No, I wouldn't," Will said firmly. "I'm on nights this week. You'll be fine here. Doc's a good watchdog. Lindsey—Miss Fox—can lend you a nightgown, and I expect she has an extra toothbrush."

"Oh, I have the essentials in my bag," MaryMar said. "Really, I don't want to trouble Lindsey."

"It's no trouble," I lied, still processing that Will was working nights now. That was something else he'd neglected to mention. "I'll take the sofa."

"It's settled, then," Will said. "Lindsey knows how to reach me. Or in an emergency, call 911. I'll give y'all a ring in the morning and check on things." He turned directly to MaryMar. "I'm real sorry about your friend."

MaryMar looked blank for a second, then remembered her role as the bereaved. Her bottom lip trembled. "Oh, I just don't know what I'll do without Lorna."

As usual, it was all about MaryMar. "Here," I said, gesturing toward my bedroom. "Make yourself at home while I take Doc out for a bathroom break."

Doc already had moved from the heater to the front door in anticipation. He headed for his favorite pine tree as I walked with Will toward the Chevy SUV emblazoned with the Granville County logo, a recent acquisition that Sheriff Griggs had squeezed out of the county commission.

"At last," Will said, once we were away from the porch light. He leaned down to kiss me. "I missed you." I started to say something like, "If you missed me so much, why didn't you call?" but my mouth was otherwise occupied. When at last we pulled away from each other, Will said, "I wish I could stay, but MaryMar turning up changes this whole investigation. We'll talk later." He dropped a quick kiss on my head.

"You never said if anything was stolen from the Simmons house."

I could see Will's grin in the light from the open door as he climbed in. "Now, that was strange. It seems the only thing missing was Elise's bathrobe."

"Oops!" I smiled as I watched him pull away into the darkness, then whistled for Doc to follow me inside.

MaryMar had taken my words literally, shutting herself in my room. I knocked on the door. "Yes?" She managed to look both demure and sexy in a pink, lacy Victoria's Secret number with silky tap pants. I hoped she was planning to take off her makeup before snuggling up in my bed.

"I thought you might need this." I held out the thick terry-cloth robe. "And I need to get a few things." I snagged two pillows from the bottom of the pile and the down duvet folded at the foot of the bed. Let her wear the robe if she got cold. I added my toothbrush, toothpaste, and contact-lens case to my precariously balanced bundle. There were clean towels in the hall bathroom—no heat, though. It was a good thing I had on socks. "Will you hand me that T-shirt over there, please?"

MaryMar picked up the oversized yellow garment my brother, Jack, had given me and read the inscription. " 'Cheese Club of Grater Orlando.' Grater is misspelled," she said. "An *e* is missing."

"It's a joke," I explained. "You know, cheese grater."

She stared at me. "Oh."

"The thing you grate cheese with."

"Oh."

I gave up. "There's another quilt on top of the cedar chest if you get cold." I thought about explaining the intricacies of the gas heater but decided it was beyond her. If I didn't mention the heater, she'd leave it alone, and I wouldn't have an asphyxiated house guest in the morning.

Bonnie and Mam looked at me sympathetically when I recounted the T-shirt incident.

"Women like that give blondes a bad name," Bonnie said, shaking her own expertly highlighted tresses.

"All women," Mam said. "I can't figure out if she's putting on some kind of act, or if she really is lacking when it comes to brains."

"She's smart enough to use her other assets," Bonnie said. "Look at all those men the other night hanging around her. You can't tell me they were interested in that snake."

"You're right," I said, opening the last package of graham crackers I kept at Pinckney for mornings when I didn't have time for breakfast. "If you dare criticize her to most men, they just assume you're jealous."

"But not all men, thank goodness," Bonnie said, reaching for the crackers. "Will seemed pretty immune to her charms, and she was laying it on thick. I wonder what's going on with her and Ron Simmons. He's lots older."

"But he doesn't look it," Mam put in. "His hair's white, but his eyebrows are dark. Both he and Ray take after their daddy, but Ron's stockier."

I nodded. If Ron's younger brother, Ray, looked like a hawk, than Ron was an eagle. "He has presence."

"Money, too, don't forget." Mam sighed. "Also a wife, but he has a reputation for forgetting her. He won't divorce Elise, though, because she'd take him to the cleaners."

"Maybe Elise is the one stalking MaryMar," Bonnie ventured.

"Or she's hired a private investigator to get the goods on MaryMar and Ron, and the threatening notes are a diversion," Mam said.

"If there are threatening notes." The cousins hadn't spent as much time as I had with MaryMar. "For all we know, MaryMar could have made the whole thing up, or even sent the notes to herself as a publicity stunt."

"No, I don't think so." Mam took Bonnie's coffee cup and rinsed it.

"The faint may have been a put-on, but she really seemed scared. And Lorna is dead. I'd be scared, too."

"Ditto," Bonnie said, shivering. "With someone watching you, you're always having to look over your shoulder. It creeps me out. It's as bad as ghosts."

"Are y'all talking ghosts again?" Posey, looming in the hall doorway, startled us. I wondered how long he'd been there. But his mention of ghosts reminded me.

"Cissy says she heard someone in the shrubbery late yesterday afternoon when she was locking up," I told Posey. "Was anybody working then?"

"No." Posey frowned. "I saw Turner Hickey down near the landing in his Jon boat 'bout midafternoon, but I don't think he'd come up here looking for that ghost gator of his."

"Ghost gator?" Bonnie asked.

"Turner thinks that old Gullah story about a white alligator haunting the Indigo marsh might have a basis in fact. He believes there's an albino gator out there," I said, handing my glass to Margaret Ann and tossing the now-empty cracker package in the trash can. So much for breakfast. "He wants it for the Gatortorium."

"I've never heard of albino alligators," Bonnie said. "Is there any such thing?"

Mam nodded. "We saw a picture of one on the Internet they found in Florida. It looked like something out of a horror movie. If you think alligators are ugly, you should see this thing—gray-white with red eyes."

"Turner is obsessed with tracking it down, like Captain Ahab and Moby-Dick," I said.

" 'Call me Ishmael,' " Bonnie intoned. "Tom loves that book."

Mam picked up the ringing phone. "Pinckney Plantation. Oh, good morning, Miss Augusta. How are you—" She scrunched up her face as she listened, trying to get a word in. "That's good. Yes, ma'am, I'll tell her. And I'll tell Marietta and Posey about—" She waited. "Bye, now. You take care."

"New marching orders?" I said, standing up. I needed to go to the attic and fetch that dratted teapot before we opened to the public.

"I guess." Mam looked perplexed. "She said for you not to bother with the teapot anymore. And I'm supposed to tell y'all"— she nodded at Posey and Marietta, who had just come into the kitchen—"that the new bed will be delivered this afternoon. What new bed?"

"One of them fancy ones like in the hospital that you can move up and down, only it looks like a regular bed." Marietta wiped off the already spotless kitchen counter. "She wants it for when she home from Bayview." She looked at Posey. "You think it gonna fit through that door?"

"What door?" I said. Miss Augusta's private rooms were on Pinckney's second floor, but she'd had trouble with the steep staircase even before her recent illness. I had a sudden vision of her ensconced in a bed behind the ropes in the back parlor, telling tourists to keep to the runners on the heart-pine floors.

"The Coach House door," Marietta said. "Miss Augusta gonna live there. There's no stairs to speak of, and it got a kitchen and a bathroom."

"The Coach House!" Mam was aghast. "But that's where we're having the rehearsal dinner, and it's headquarters for the wedding reception. We can't have a reclining bed in the middle of the room!"

"Why not?" Bonnie chuckled. "It'll give people something to talk about. And Sue Beth and Wiley could save on their honeymoon."

"Hush that foolishness, child," Marietta admonished. "You gonna to upset your sister. Miss Augusta's not moving back till after the wedding."

"We'll store the bed in the stable," Posey said. "There's room now that Miss Augusta's old Caddy is gone. Just the truck and the golf cart."

"Aw, shucks," Bonnie said. "I was looking forward to scattering rose petals on the bridal bower."

"Forget the roses." Mam picked up garden shears and a battered peach basket from by the back door. "I need your help greening in the centerpieces so I can put the flowers in tomorrow. We need to cut some pittosporum and see what else we can find. Lindsey, are you coming?"

"Y'all go on. I need to clear up some stuff in the office." I'd rather tackle the tour-guide script than muck about outside in the damp grass and bushes. "Watch out for snakes."

Margaret Ann flinched as she opened the door. "Here, Bonnie, you go first."

Posey followed me into the office off the kitchen. "I need to show you something," he said, fishing out some folded papers from his dark green work pants. "These are the receipts for the gardening supplies and fertilizer I picked up last week from the feed-and-seed. I've been meaning to bring them in here from the truck for the file, but I keep forgetting. Good thing, too."

"How come?" I switched on the computer at my desk.

"Because three bags of fertilizer, some weed-killer, and other stuff are missing."

He had my full attention now. "Where from?"

"The little shed by the new graveyard."

Which was actually the old graveyard, but I knew what he meant. The Pinckney family plot was a gated enclave near the chapel not far from the plantation's main entrance. But we'd recently discovered a slave cemetery in the woods, apparently built on an ancient Indian burial mound. Archaeologists from several of the state colleges already had formed a team to excavate the area this summer. Meanwhile, Posey had erected a toolshed by the roped-off site and was clearing away the dense underbrush to make a path from one of the back roads.

"Not many people know that shed even exists," I said.

"I know, and we don't usually keep much in there. Besides which, the latch is broken. I only put the overflow in this time because the main shed's full of flowerpots and those chandeliers."

"For the wedding. Margaret Ann had J. T. haul them over a couple weeks ago. I thought she was going to put them in that annex to the stable."

"The torches are in there, and the lanterns."

"But of course." I sighed. My cousin and this wedding were out of control. "Let me ask Mam if for any reason she 'borrowed' anything. Remember, she used all that spray paint on those lanterns. And then she took the hoses."

"Yeah, but I think we'd have heard if she got anything out the shed."

I raised my eyebrows in question.

" 'Cause there's a blacksnake that lives underneath that hustles out whenever there's company."

I grinned. "It would serve her right for picking up hoses that don't belong to her."

CHAPTER TEN

Kudzu Gets a Bad Rap

"It's just not right! In fact, I think it's downright tacky."

"Bonnie, it'll be fine. You'll see. Here, Lindsey, what do you think?"

I looked up from a South Carolina history book to see my cousins standing in the office doorway, Margaret Ann holding a peach basket full of greenery.

"Is that kudzu?"

"Would you believe it?" Bonnie said. "Mam wants to use it in the arrangements for the wedding."

"Hey, the leaves are pretty and green, and I don't know why people don't like kudzu anyway. There's sure enough of it."

"That's why." I closed the book. No way was I going to be able to concentrate on the economics of Low Country plantations. Besides, this promised to be more interesting than indigo, rice, and sea-island cotton. "Kudzu grows about a foot a day and chokes everything in sight. If you don't keep your windows shut, it'll come in and strangle you while you sleep."

"Pooh. That's an old wives' tale." Mam considered the contents of her basket. "Spanish moss is worse. It's got those little bugs in it. Kudzu gets a bad rap. This dark green will be pretty with the purple hydrangeas."

"I thought those hydrangeas were white," I said.

"I'll spray them," Mam said cheerfully. "How do you think florists match all those horrible colors on those tiny magazine pictures brides bring in? Anyway, hydrangeas tint beautifully."

"If you say so, but I still think kudzu is common." Bonnie wrinkled her nose.

"Then I won't use any on your casket spray."

"Yeah, like you're going to outlive me, big sister. Some Southern princess bride is going to finish you off when she finds kudzu in her bouquet."

"Oh, hush! I wouldn't put it in a bouquet," Mam said. "But you're right that those princess brides may be the death of me."

"They aren't just bred in the South, though," I put in. "Tell Bonnie about the wedding you did a couple weeks ago."

"Oh, shoot, she was from Chicago, and she was so used to the cold that she didn't think anything about an outdoor plantation wedding in March. It was thirty-five the day of the wedding! I like to froze setting up. We had heaters for the tents and all. Still, that wasn't the worst. She wanted me to plant gardenia bushes under the tents to make it look more like outdoors. Plant them!"

"Did you?"

"No way. I just ordered a hundred out-of-season gardenias from California and floated them in large candle bowls. She paid an arm and a leg for that, or her daddy did. She's his little princess."

"They call them bridezillas on that cable show," Bonnie said. "I like princess brides better."

"I was at this wedding planners' convention last year with some Yankee florists, and they'd never heard the term before," Mam said. "I asked didn't they have hissy-fit-throwing brides that need to have every itty-bitty thing just so. And they said yes, but they just call them bitches!" She clapped a hand over her mouth. "You're not going to charge me a nickel for that, are you, Lindsey? It was a quote."

I smiled. "I already owe you so much I ought to charge you double 'cause it wasn't a slip of the tongue." Now that I'm no longer in a newsroom, I don't cuss nearly as much as I used to, but Margaret Ann's still making money off me. And more often than not, it's because of something she drags me into. "Hey," I remembered, "you haven't borrowed any more gardening stuff since last week, have you?"

"No, but I'm going to see if Posey has some extra lantern fuel in case we need it for the wedding. It can go on Beth's bill. That's not a problem, is it?"

"No, no problem." Other than that I now had to worry about a thief on the plantation, I might have added. I'd talk to Posey after lunch. The main security gate was working fine, but there was access to the posted acres through little-known dirt roads, including one I'd found near Middle House. "But we do need to go check on our problem bridesmaid. She called awhile ago asking if I was going to bring her lunch."

Bonnie chuckled. "She's a princess, all right."

"She's a royal pain in the ass," I said before I could stop myself.

"Lindsey Lee Fox!" Margaret Ann crowed. "You owe me another nickel."

"MaryMar, we're home!" Mam caroled as I opened the front door.

Doc barreled into me like I'd been gone for years, then leaped down the steps past Bonnie, zipping toward his pine-tree pit stop. I'd leave him out while we ate lunch. There hadn't been time this morning for our usual long walk on the beach.

Everyone was in the kitchen. Bonnie had her head in the refrigerator, and Mam was putting slices of wheat bread on four plates on the counter. MaryMar was sitting at the table in the white robe, legs crossed, wet hair wrapped in a blue towel. I noticed she'd repainted her toenails—rose pink this time.

"I assume no one called." I'd left a note by the phone saying to let the machine pick up.

"Actually, Major McLeod did. He woke me up, so I hadn't read your note yet. He told me not to answer again because he still wants me to stay hidden while he continues the investigation." MaryMar looked sulky but then conceded, "He was real nice about it, though, and said I shouldn't worry, that everything was being done to protect me. Say, didn't I hear he's gotten a divorce? Is he seeing anybody now?"

"He's seeing Lindsey," Mam blurted. If looks could kill, Mam would have been dead on the kitchen floor, but my stare didn't faze her. "They're in *luvv*." She drew out the sound.

Geez, Louise. She couldn't keep her trap shut to save her life.

"Oh." Mary Mar considered a cuticle before she looked at me, an enigmatic smile tugging at her lips. "Congratulations."

Bonnie saved me by emerging from the refrigerator with her hands full. "Here's the Duke's, the mustard, and the ham. There's Miracle Whip, too, and lettuce, if anybody wants it. What about you, MaryMar?"

"I don't much care for ham," MaryMar said. "I usually eat sushi for lunch."

Mam made a face. "I like my seafood cooked. Sushi always reminds me of bait."

"There's tuna in the pantry," I said. "But if you open the pouch, I'll need to put Peaches in my room. He can smell it a mile away. Where is he, anyway?"

"If you mean the cat, he kept nosing around when I was trying to do my nails—I borrowed your polish, by the way—so I put him in that bathroom where you have his litter box." MaryMar sniffed. "It needs changing."

"On my list," I said, irked that she'd used my polish—which meant she'd been opening drawers—and locked up my cat. Still, I wasn't as miffed as Peaches. I'd rescue him with some treats after we ate. "Ham, tuna, PBJ?"

MaryMar winced. "Ham is fine. Is that sweet tea?"

"In the green pitcher," I said. "Water's in the blue. Bonnie, the chips are in the pantry. I moved everything from the top of the fridge after Peaches decided it made a nice perch."

"I wouldn't have thought he could get up there with his deformity," MaryMar said, cutting the crust off the sandwich Mam had placed in front of her.

"Peaches?" Bonnie looked up from her plate.

"He's not deformed," I said. "What are you talking about?"

"His paws are all wrong. They look like mittens."

"He has extra toes because he's a Hemingway cat."

"They raise deformed cats in Hemingway?"

Mam almost choked as her tea went down the wrong way. Bonnie's jaw dropped.

"Not the town in South Carolina," I said. "Hemingway the writer. When Ernest Hemingway lived in Key West, he had all these five-toed cats. A bunch of them are still there. There was a story on Hemingway cats in *Perfect Pet* the same issue with Watson on the cover."

MaryMar's lip curled in distaste. "I guess I'm really not an animal person. Lorna wanted to get one of those little rat dogs, but I told her I didn't want it yapping around the apartment."

The sisters and I exchanged looks. None of us was much on fu-fu dogs, but still . . .

"Maybe she was lonely." Bonnie voiced our thoughts. "We heard she has no people. Did she have any close friends besides you? A boyfriend?"

MaryMar shook her head. "No, no. She swore off men after her husband was killed, said they were more trouble than they were worth. I tried to tell her that not all men are like Dale Spivey—what a loser!— but she claimed she wasn't interested." She patted her mouth with a napkin, then folded it beside her plate. "To tell you the truth, Lorna was different from when we were in high school. Back then, she was a lot of fun, always up for a good time. Just the usual stuff, though— cutting class, sneaking out at night, drinking beer by the railroad tracks. I kept telling her she was doing her complexion no favors smoking all those cigarettes, but she just laughed." MaryMar touched her napkin again. "She quit smoking when she was in the clinic—quit everything, I guess. Most nights, she shut herself in her room with her computer and the TV. Of course, I wasn't always home. We really went our own ways, mostly." MaryMar appeared to be thinking. "Y'all saw her, right? How she was dressed like me?"

"That's why we thought she was you," Bonnie said. "That and the hair."

MaryMar straightened the towel on her head. "She was good with hair, I'll give her that. But that look-alike stuff was all her idea. It started one day last month when she showed up in the same skirt I was wearing. I thought it was a coincidence, but then it happened again, and one day her hair was lots blonder."

"Did you ask her about it?" Mam said.

"Yes, and she shrugged it off, said she hoped I didn't mind, that she'd always wanted a sister, and wasn't it fun that people thought we were related. Then I felt sorry for her, and I figured there wasn't any harm, so I let it go. I had other things on my mind."

"Like the stalker." Mam shivered. "What did his letters say?"

Mam had the nerve of a bad tooth, but MaryMar wasn't bothered. "He didn't say he was going to kill me, but he made me feel, well, dirty. The letters all said the same thing: 'Smile. I'm watching you.' "

Mam cringed. "That must be just awful. Lindsey was stalked once."

"You were?" MaryMar looked at me with surprise. Obviously, I didn't rate a stalker in her book, much less a good-looking deputy.

"Yes, when I worked at a TV station in Charlotte right after college."

"You were on TV?" Her disbelief was insulting.

I held the salt shaker in front of my face like a microphone. "Lindsey Fox, Eyewitness News," I said in my best news-reporter voice, deep and serious. "Or Eyewitless, as some called it."

"But you had a stalker."

"Yes, but it wasn't letters. He left a picture of himself on the windshield of my car outside my apartment."

"So it was easy for them to catch him?" MaryMar asked.

"It wasn't a picture of his face."

"Eww," Mam said. "You never told us that part."

"It's not one of my favorite memories."

The truth was the grainy Polaroid had scared the bejesus out of me. If I hadn't been living with two roommates in an upstairs apartment with a burly retired fire chief below us, I'd have moved immediately. The police officer who took the report was reassuring, telling me that perverts like mine rarely attacked. But I had my boyfriend at the time pick me up at work for a while, and I kept a can of pepper spray and a whistle at hand.

"But they did catch him?" MaryMar asked with a note of nervousness. "They found him, right?"

"I don't know," I said. "I never got any more pictures, so maybe they did. I went to work for the newspaper not too long after that, so I wasn't on the air anymore."

"And you were never asked to identify him in a lineup," Bonnie said with a grin.

"Bonnie Lynn! This is nothing to laugh at." Mam turned to MaryMar. "I'm sure they'll find him. You're safe here. No one knows where you are."

"I know." MaryMar sighed. "Do you think I can call my agent in Atlanta? I'm up for a part in an infomercial."

"You're right, Lindsey." Bonnie fastened her seatbelt. "She's a pain in the patootie. Just when you think there's a real person there, she gets the stupids again. I hope she's right about being a size six or she's going to pop right out the top of that bridesmaid's dress."

"She's as big or bigger than you on top, Lindsey, and you can't wear a six, or even an eight."

"Thank you, Mam, for that fashion update. For your information, I have a narrow back, and there are eights in my closet."

"Which you don't wear anymore." Mam leaned up from the backseat. "In fact, I think you should just give me that red Ann Taylor."

"It's too loose up top for you," I said with some satisfaction.

"Not if I wear the right bra. And I don't see why you're so huffy. You're lucky that when you gained weight, it went to your boobs."

"Girls, girls," Bonnie said. "Lindsey, slow down. You'll land us in the marsh."

I eased up on the gas. This back route to Pinckney was a crumbling blacktop that twisted through the wetlands near Crab Creek before entering the deep woods.

A siren sliced through the air. I saw flashing lights behind me.

"See, Lindsey? Bonnie said you were going too fast."

"I wasn't speeding," I said, braking to a stop. "It's Olivia." I leaned out my window as she pulled up beside me.

"How do I get to Pinckney Landing from here?" she yelled from the Crown Vic.

"It's easiest if you just follow me," I said, picturing the web of unmarked dirt roads between us and the landing. "It's not that far, but it'll take forever to explain. What's up?"

"Go, then. Posey called dispatch to report a shooting."

"A shooting?" Mam was by my ear again as I stepped on the accelerator and signaled a left turn. "If EMS isn't with her, probably no one's hurt, or at least not bad."

"You want me to drop you off?" We were bumping along a narrow dirt road with no shoulder to speak of. "You can cut through by the slave cemetery and walk back up to Pinckney."

"Heck no," Mam said. "I want to know what's going on. Come on, Lindsey, speed up. You're going too slow."

CHAPTER ELEVEN

Miss Fortune, or In the Pink

Spring was slow in coming to this part of the island, where sunlight barely penetrated the junglelike woods. On cloudy days like this one, it was dim, even dismal. Because of all the recent rain, trees on either side of the curving road stood in a foot of still water as dark as wet pine bark. A film of lime-green pollen coated a black pool where several gnarled and broken stumps reached upward like drowning fingers.

"It's the set for a horror movie," Bonnie said. *"Return of the Swamp Thing."*

"It is spooky." Mam leaned forward again. "Are you sure you know where you're going, Lindsey? I don't remember this on any map of Pinckney."

"It's not on a map. Posey told me about it."

"You mean you've never been here before? Are you about to get us and Olivia lost? I don't want to get stuck in the mud in the middle of nowhere."

"It's not muddy, just sort of soft," I said, negotiating a water-filled dip. "And I know where I am. We're going to turn left right up there."

I would have missed the turn, though, if not for the grimy white yard statues on either side of another dirt road almost hidden by honeysuckle.

"Who in the world put Greek goddesses out here?" Bonnie peered at the moss-stained figure on her side.

"Probably whoever used to live back here. There's an old brick foundation practically buried by your precious kudzu, Mam. I think it was a gamekeeper's cottage once upon a time."

"Seems like a good place for a deer stand," Mam said.

"These woods are posted, but I expect we get some poachers. Maybe Posey's caught one."

The tunnel-like road suddenly curved into daylight. Field and marsh led to the old plantation landing and boathouse, the rotting boards weathered to silver. This had been the main entrance to Pinckney back in the days when boats and barges plied the sometimes treacherous river. Supplies and passengers were off-loaded at the dock, where horse-drawn wagons and carriages waited to make the journey to the main house and outbuildings. I'd seen enough movies to imagine the bustling scene—laborers sweating as they toted sacks of grain, smaller packages of sugar and tea, bolts of cloth, and heavy steamer trunks; young boys holding horses while fine ladies lifted their hoop skirts, mincing across the much-trodden path. Bales of sea-island cotton, the crop that had made the planters rich, would have been stacked to one side, ready for the journey to the mainland.

That was the Hollywood version, though, and I knew it wasn't the only one. Old photos showed Yankee soldiers on this same dock when Union troops occupied Indigo during the Civil War. Officers lived at Pinckney while freed slaves scratched a living from the ground, growing vegetables in what had been the rose garden. They fished the creeks, too, casting nets while the soldiers hunted game.

More than a century had passed, but there was something timeless about the picture that presented itself to us now. Two men—one black, one white—leaned on the dock's old rails, looking at the mud flats where blue crabs dallied in the shallows. A slight wind rippled pewter water that seemed to merge into the gray sky. A lone seagull sailed overhead. Tied to a water oak overhanging the creek bank, a green metal Jon boat gently shifted on the incoming tide. A clump of cassina bushes partially obscured the landing itself, the sloping concrete slick with pluff mud. Oyster shells grew up the sides of the ramp like jagged teeth.

Posey was in conversation with Turner Hickey, who had his hands in his pockets. Turner was a generation older, but age and race were no hindrance to a couple of bubbas talking hunting and fishing. They looked up at the sound of our arrival and ambled over to where we parked at road's end.

"They don't either one look too concerned." Mam sounded disappointed as she opened the car door.

" 'Bout time you showed up," Posey drawled to Olivia.

"You told dispatch it wasn't an emergency," she said. "And you better not be wasting my time." Her grin took any sting out of her words. She and Posey were cousins somewhere along the line.

"I made him call," Turner said, nodding at the three of us. "Somebody shot at me up round the bend. Got my boat. Come see."

What we saw was a dime-sized hole about three inches above the water line.

"You think maybe it was a stray shot from some hunter?" Olivia knelt for a closer examination.

"Maybe, but there were two shots. The first one got the boat. I felt the whack when the bullet hit the side, then heard the shot itself. Then something went whizzing past my head. I didn't stick around for a third shot. I hunkered down and hightailed it out of there."

"Where exactly was this?" I asked. "Were you still near Pinckney or closer to the waterway?" I was worried. Cissy's intruder at the house was bad enough, but gunshots—stray or otherwise—were even worse. The plantation didn't need that kind of publicity just as the tourist season was getting into swing.

Turner pointed off to the northeast. "See that grove of pines beyond those needle palms? If you go past there, there's a shallow creek that turns into swamp."

Posey nodded. "That's Pinckney. There's nothing over there, though, 'cept marsh and swamp. And gators. I've heard a couple of bulls roar during mating season."

"That's why I was there," Turner said. "I was hoping I might spot him."

"Him?" Olivia asked. "You mean that ghost gator? I thought you'd given up on him after all this time."

"He's around here, I'm sure of it. I know y'all think I'm crazy, but I'm gonna find him. He's not a ghost, and it weren't no ghost taking potshots at me."

"I can see." Olivia stood. "Let me get the camera and take a picture of that bullet hole. Then I'll call in and write up a report. Somebody will be in touch. You going back to Cottonmouth?"

"Naw. I put in at White's Landing." He jumped gracefully from the bank into the bow of the boat. As soon as Olivia snapped a couple of pictures, Posey untied the rope and threw it to Turner, who waved good-bye. "See you folks later. Thanks for the help."

The boat caught the current, its motor sputtering. We watched it round the curve, where it seemed to fade right into the marsh.

Olivia turned to Posey. "Is there any road access back where he was?"

"Not so you can tell, but I haven't been up that way in a while." Posey pointed past the boathouse. "That's sweet grass over there, which is why I came down to the landing. Marietta said she's 'bout run out, and she wanted to finish a last Easter basket. It's getting harder and harder to find sweet grass up near Mount Pleasant. I hear people are combing the islands, there's such demand. Could be there's some in that creek area, but I can't see anyone shooting somebody over sweet grass."

"Not until it's turned into a basket, at least." Mam looked where Posey had pointed. "Prices have really gone up the last five years. I know Sue Beth thought about having little sweet-grass baskets for the bridesmaids instead of the brandy snifters, but even a bitty one costs about twenty-five dollars now."

"That's because it takes hours to make even the small ones," Olivia said. "It's hard, too, that weaving. Marietta tried to teach all us girls when we were growing up, but I didn't take to it."

I nodded. "We want to teach classes, once we get the interpretive center at Pinckney up and running. It really is a dying art."

I cherish my several sweet-grass baskets, but Mam is the real collector. A half-dozen of her intricately woven miniatures, gifts lovingly made by her students' grandmothers, are on display at the historical museum. We'd recently pooled resources to buy a lidded basket as a wedding present for Sue Beth. "She can't get this at Pottery Barn," Mam had noted, "and she's island girl enough to know it."

"Are you still planning on putting the interpretive center down here?" Bonnie asked.

"We're thinking about it," I said. "Posey's got plans for a nature trail, and this seems like a logical place because of the creek and all the different trees. How many kinds of palms did you tell me, Posey?"

"Going on a dozen." He gestured toward the boathouse. "There's dwarf palmetto and cabbage palm right there. Windmill palm, too. It's sometimes called China palm because it's native to China. Its Latin name is *Trachycarpus fortunie*, after the great plant explorer Robert Fortune. And that feathery-looking one is a jelly palm. It flowers in late June and fruits in August."

"You can eat the fruit, right?" Bonnie asked. "What's it taste like?"

"Not like chicken," I said. "It's kind of a mix of pineapple and banana. You can make jelly out of it. Aunt Cora has."

"I better get a move on," Olivia said, heading toward her cruiser. "Posey, Lindsey, y'all show me on the map where Turner was talking about."

Mam and Bonnie went to look at the jelly palm. Olivia spread out a map of Indigo on the hood of her car so we could see all the creeks threading through the pear-shaped island. Posey's brown finger immediately found the plantation's river landing. He traced the river north toward the Intracoastal Waterway, stopping at a small inlet.

Olivia marked the map with a pencil. "I might ride over near there and see if there are any tracks from a Jeep or an ATV."

Mam called from near the boathouse. "Hey, Posey, come tell us what this plant is. It might work as greenery, but I don't want to up-root baby palms."

Posey walked toward the sisters. Olivia bit her bottom lip as she stared at the map. "Lindsey, do you know if the plantation electric bill has been higher than usual?"

"The new one should be here this week. Why?"

"I have an idea."

"About Pinckney's power bill?"

"Maybe." Olivia pointed her pencil at the map. "Meth labs need a fair amount of power, and it could be that someone's tapping into the plantation's lines. A utility bill tipped off that bust north of Centerville last month. The property owner was out of town, and he was madder than a wet hen when he got socked for a couple hundred extra. They found the meth lab in a rusty trailer he was using for fertilizer and yard equipment, conveniently enough."

"How so?"

"Because some of the ingredients needed to cook up meth are available at your local hardware store or feed-and-seed, like the ammonia in fertilizer," Olivia said.

"We're missing some supplies, including fertilizer. Posey told me yesterday. He was going to check to see if maybe they were misplaced. You want to talk to him about it?"

Olivia eyed Posey speculatively. He was crouched, holding back some bushes so Bonnie and Mam could see beneath their leafy over-hang. "I'll catch him later, if I find anything over there," she said. "It's just an idea, although it might explain the shots fired at Turner."

I nodded. "He's been hunting that ghost gator all over the place. But wouldn't it be stupid to call attention to yourself by firing a gun?"

"Meth doesn't make you smart. It just rots your mind and your teeth," Olivia said. "We ought to get on this pretty quick. It might be those same guys from Sunset. They could already be moving the lab somewhere else. Those shots may have bought them some time."

I remembered something from my research on Pinckney. "There used to be a lot of illegal stills on Indigo during Prohibition and even after. People said the best moonshine came from Pinckney."

Olivia folded the map. "Bootlegging's back big time, only now it's meth instead of whiskey. Don't say anything to Posey until I talk to the boss." That would be Will. "I don't want Posey or anyone else to try to track down a meth lab. It's too dangerous. The department's getting ready to send out some alerts to property owners and land-lords about how to spot possible labs and meth users. It's important to stay away from them until we investigate. The alerts should be back from the printer by the end of the week. But we're not set up quite yet to take calls from every nosy neighbor who thinks the guy next door is making meth just because he bought a jumbo box of coffee filters from Costco."

"I sure hope you're wrong about this," I said. "I don't think meth labs are on Miss Augusta's list of approved tourist attractions at Pinckney."

⁓

As I left Pinckney, the late-afternoon shadows were lengthening, the trees casting stripes across the road. Thanks to Posey, I was able to identify a scruffy China palm, its fronds tipped with brown. Having grown up with palmettos, I'd always taken them for granted as part of the island's jungle landscape. Five hours to the north in Charlotte, where I'd lived before returning to Indigo, homeowners occasionally planted small palms to give their yards an exotic touch, but the trees looked out of place in the subdivisions that grew like kudzu in the red clay.

I'd been back going on three months, but I still wasn't used to living on the island again after all those years. I kept feeling like I was caught in Brigadoon while my real life continued in the city without me. Some-times, I woke in the night surprised to find myself in Miss Maudie's front room and not my old duplex. I had a new job, a new dog, and a new relationship. Mam said Will and I were in love, but she didn't know we'd been there before. Were my feelings now mixed up with those from the past? My new life was familiar and strange all at once.

Take this evening. In Charlotte, I might have met friends for dinner and maybe gone to a movie. Or I might have picked up takeout on my way home from the magazine office and curled up with a book. I had options. Here, it was an hour's drive to the nearest multiplex. And if you wanted Chinese—which I suddenly did—well, China Palace didn't deliver twenty-five miles.

What was Will's official SUV doing in my driveway? Why hadn't he called ahead? Rats. No doubt, Miss Prisspot was in there with her clean, shining hair and newly manicured nails, while bedraggled me looked like the dog's dinner. Still, as Mam had pointed out, I had comparable assets in one regard. I squared my shoulders and thrust my chest forward as I opened the front door.

The smell of Chinese food led me straight to the dining room. Will and MaryMar sat at one end of the table, empty plates and boxes of China Palace takeout between them. Peaches and Doc hovered at their feet, hoping for some Kung Pao Chicken.

"Hey!" MaryMar was all smiles. She looked fetching in my favorite pink oxford-cloth shirt and a pair of jeans I hadn't been able to zip up in two years. "I forgot to tell you that when Major McLeod—Will—called, he said he'd bring us dinner. We went ahead and started without you. There's plenty here. We saved your fortune cookie, too."

"Thanks." I just bet she forgot to tell me—on purpose. And I didn't need a fortune cookie to see that I was in for another long evening. "But I want to take Doc for a run before I eat."

Will stood. "You go ahead and eat. I'll take him before I go back on duty."

"There's no need for anyone to go." MaryMar held out her egg-roll-sticky fingers to Doc, who obligingly licked them. "He and I went for a long walk this afternoon."

My "You did?" and Will's surprised "Where did you go?" came out simultaneously.

"Down to White's Landing."

"You were supposed to stay here, out of sight." Will looked grim. "Did you see anybody, or did anybody see you?"

"Well, a few," MaryMar said, her blue eyes wide. "But it was all people I know. Mike Bishop lives down there, and he looks after Ron's boat for him. His little yellow boat is docked next to the *Do Ron Ron*. And your cousin's husband—what's his name, J. T.?—was putting a Jon boat in. He waved."

Oh, Mam was going to love hearing about J. T. playing hooky from his job as a sales manager for a pharmaceutical firm to go fishing for the last of the winter trout.

"Anybody else?"

"That bug van was driving down the road as I was coming back. The driver waved." MaryMar's brow furrowed. "Oh, and Scott was there waiting on Turner."

"Scott?" Will puzzled over the name.

"Russo," I said. "He's the photographer for Sue Beth's wedding."

"Scott does a lot of Charleston weddings and parties, as well as wildlife photography. I've known him for ages. I saw him a couple weeks ago at a charity shindig for sick kids. At least I think it was sick kids. Might have been the halfway house for reformed prisoners. My agent, Jason, sets up all my personal appearances." She turned from Will to me. "I couldn't get Jason on the phone today, so I just left a message for him to call me here."

Will is pretty even tempered, but when he gets mad, his eyes turn this sort of icy blue and his whole face tenses. "You let her use the phone to call her agent?"

"Hey, don't get on me!" It was my turn to be mad. "I'm not her keeper. It's not my fault if she's acting like she wants this stalker to find her."

"Oh, I don't!" MaryMar was all innocence. "How could you even think that?" Her bottom lip trembled. "Does this mean I can't stay here?" Did I detect a hint of hope? Had she planned this whole scenario? "Does this mean I'll need to go with you?" She looked beseechingly at Will.

He lasered in on her. "You'll have to go somewhere. Lindsey, too."

MaryMar was no more surprised than I was. "Me? I'm not being stalked."

"But she was down at the landing in your clothes with your dog.

We have to assume word will get out that she's here. I'm not leaving you alone in this house, in case someone does come looking for her."

"Oh, I'll be fine," I said. "Can't you put her in protective custody or something?"

"The something's what I've got to figure out, for both of you." Will rubbed his jaw. I could almost hear him gritting his teeth.

"We could go to Mama and Daddy's on the beach. They're not there." If I was going to be kicked out of my house, I could at least go sleep in my old bedroom.

"No, that's almost as bad as here. You'd still be isolated, plus that's the first place someone might think of."

"Pinckney?" I offered, although I didn't relish the thought of bunking in Miss Augusta's four-poster near the attic stairs. "We have the security gate."

"And maybe intruders, from what Olivia reported. Let me think. MaryMar, you might as well go and collect your things. I'll help Lindsey with these dishes."

Mary Mar swished off to my bedroom.

"Don't I even get to eat?" I picked at some fried rice clinging to the top of one of the cartons. It was cold but still good.

Will's face relaxed into an almost-smile. "That's the Lindsey I know, wondering where her next meal's coming from." He picked up a white cartons's wire hanger with one finger. "It's takeout. You can take it with you."

"Where to?"

"I'm going to make a phone call and fix that up." He looked toward my room. There was no beautiful blonde in sight. He touched my hair and smiled. "I'm sorry you have to move, but I can't have anything happen to you. And I shouldn't have blamed you for MaryMar being an idiot."

"Mmm," I said, slightly mollified. I didn't think it was to my benefit to point out that MaryMar was a scheming little so-and-so. At least he thought she was several ants short of a picnic.

Will realized he hadn't quite made up for his cozy dinner with the glamour puss. His lips brushed my hair. "You know," he whispered in my ear, "you look so much better in that pink shirt than she does."

CHAPTER TWELVE

Lost Sleep and Lost Beach

Pink brushed the eastern sky as I stood on Mam and J. T.'s dock. If the sunrise had any say in the matter, it was going to be a beautiful day on Indigo.

I groaned. I felt like a train wreck. Will's brilliant idea of a safe house had turned out to be my cousin's home on Fishing Creek. Will figured that since J. T. had already seen MaryMar at the landing, the poor guy should now be trusted to help protect her. J. T. is a man of few words, probably because Mam's never short of them. He'd just nodded as Will explained the situation, walking him out to the SUV. As for Mam, she was thrilled to be in the middle of things again ("I'm sorry the house stinks, but we had fish for supper") and immediately had Cissy vacate her room for MaryMar. "Cissy can share with Bonnie," she'd said. "It's right across the hall from her room and next to us."

Which meant the den couch for me, both Doc and Peaches vying to share my sleeping space. Will had told me to bring them, too. "We don't know when it'll be safe for you to go home," he said. "Besides, Thursday's your day off from Pinckney, so y'all can stay inside, out of sight. You can help Margaret Ann with those wedding flowers."

The idea of being cooped up all day with MaryMar making

corsages was hardly my idea of time off. "Don't you think someone might figure out that if I'm not at Middle House, MaryMar would be with me here?" I asked, trying not to beg. "I need to research my next *Perfect Pet* story. The Caseys are raising a shepherd puppy until she's old enough for guide-dog school."

"Which won't be for several months." Will's jaw had tightened. "The story can wait. Really, I want y'all here. J. T.'s got a good alarm system wired right into dispatch ever since they had that break-in last fall when someone was looking for drug samples."

All the burglars had found was Mam's Tylenol PM. I wished now that I'd thought to take some before going to bed. Still miffed at MaryMar and Will—he was so darned nice to her I could kick him— I'd tossed and turned all night. My sleep had been further troubled by a thunderstorm. Peaches and Doc—joined by Mam's black-and-white cocker, Chloe—had insisted the couch was big enough for us all.

"Thanks a lot, you guys," I muttered now as the dogs frisked in the yard behind me. Lost sleep makes me cranky.

"Lost Beach," Mam said, thrusting a cold Coke can into my hand.

"What about it?" I grumbled, taking a long drink. It was going to take more than one Coke to get my engine going. Mam, of course, was revved and ready for the day, dressed in faded khakis and a long-sleeved navy top.

"We're going to Lost Beach. I thought of it as soon as I heard the thunder last night. There's always great shells there after a high tide and a storm. I woke up Bonnie, and she's drinking her coffee now. Go finish getting dressed. And don't forget a hat. There are extras by the door."

"What about MaryMar?" The caffeine was beginning to penetrate my morning haze.

"What about her?" Mam was busying herself in the boathouse, banging two buckets together. I wished she'd stop. "Let Sleeping Beauty lie. We're not the ones under house arrest. Cissy's sleeping in, and so's J. T. He's going to Columbia this afternoon and staying over till tomorrow. I think he planned it so he wouldn't be here while I'm doing flowers."

I was positive that was his plan. The closer Mam gets to a dead-line, the tighter she's wound. "But if you need to do flowers, why are we going shelling?"

"We need shells for the wedding." Mam dragged a couple of can-vas tote bags from a corner.

"Do you mean you're going to put shells in the bridesmaids' fish-bowls, too?"

"Of course not. That would be silly. I'm putting them in the tulip bowls." She kicked a crab trap out of her way. "The bowls are large, with a separate glass cylinder in the center. I'm putting white French tulips in the center and seashells in the other part. Won't that look pretty?"

"I guess," I said, draining the Coke.

"Then I'm putting them on the food table at the reception," Mam continued without coming up for air. "I have three bowls, so I need lots of little shells."

"Whatever. I need more Coke."

"I already put some drinks in the cooler. And we'll take the dogs with us."

Mam, as usual, had planned everything before even brushing her teeth. I had bed hair and was still wearing the T-shirt I'd slept in. Bonnie was standing in the kitchen, a cup of coffee in one hand and a glazed expression on her face. Peaches hopped on a barstool at the counter and patiently waited, as if he were at a diner for his morning meal. Smart cat. He knew caffeine came before kibble.

"We're going to Lost Beach," I told Bonnie, who still hadn't moved.

"So I hear," she mumbled. "I'm trying to think positive thoughts, like we might find some sea glass. The pretty blue kind." She yawned.

"Don't do that. It's contagious. You might as well put on your shoes. I'll be ready in just a minute, as soon as I feed Peaches. We need to get out of here while the getting's good, before you-know-who is awake."

"I'm awake." She yawned again. "I think."

"Do you think it's a good idea to take J. T.'s boat?" I warily eyed the gleaming white seventeen-foot Sea Fox with its matching ivory Johnson motor.

"He hasn't cleaned the Jon boat after his little fishing trip yesterday," Mam said, taking the cooler from me and stowing it on board. "That's the deal. Whoever uses the boat cleans it and the catch, and the other one cooks. I cooked."

She settled into the driver's seat at the stern, Bonnie riding shotgun. Both dogs were in the bow, noses sniffing, tails wagging. I sat on the middle console as the motor purred to life. Mam took it easy through the winding creek, past the No Wake signs posted on her neighbors' docks. But as we neared the mouth of the river, she sped up. The boat bounced when we hit the open water. "There might be some chop!" Mam yelled redundantly as we smacked the whitecaps. "Whoo-ee! Lost Beach or bust!"

Lost Beach wasn't really lost, just a little displaced. Once part of Indigo, it had provided a respite from the hot weather for the island's planters, who retreated to beach cottages during the summer months. But the great hurricane of 1893 had washed away all the houses and cut off the beach from the tip of Indigo, where the river emptied into the sea. Now, a channel separated the island from the islet and its deserted beach. Swimming across looked possible, if you ignored the Danger signs and the name of the channel—Drowning Creek. But the shore opposite Indigo was a formidable, snake-infested jungle. If you made the swim, you'd still need a machete to cut across to Lost Beach. The good news was you could reach it by boat from the ocean side.

We hit a swell, and the dogs scrambled to stay upright. They were better sailors than me. I was beginning to wish I hadn't drunk the Coke so fast. The sun wasn't bright yet, but the air was warmer than I expected on the water. March weather on Indigo can bring most anything, including snow. Tornadoes are possible, or storms with high spring tides. Hurricane season runs June through November, but a nasty nor'easter might pound the beach with driving rain and heavy surf. Then again, we spent some prom weekends getting our first sunburns of the year. You never know if the weather will be wild or mild. March madness.

Mam slowed as we came round the side of Lost Beach, a strip of gray-white sand bordered by woods. Because the tide was high, we wouldn't have to climb far to get up out of the water. If I jumped, I might not get wet at all. Still, I rolled up my khakis. The dogs were already splashing in the shallows.

"Wait!" Mam called. "Grab the buckets, Lindsey. Then jump out so Bonnie and I can pull the boat up high and anchor it on the beach. The tide is going out, I think, but we won't be here so long that we'll have to push it out much when we're ready to leave."

My jump fell short, and my left foot went in. The cool water filled my Ked. At least I hadn't worn socks. Wet socks are the worst. Okay, maybe not as bad as famine or plague or the dead horseshoe crab we were downwind of, but you know what I mean.

"It's kind of high for shelling," Bonnie said, putting the cooler above the tide line and well away from the crab carcass. "Erosion's getting this beach, too. Lost Beach may be really lost before too long."

Mam set off to our left. "We can still get some shells up here near the reeds while we wait out the tide."

I took off my Keds, tied them together, and hung them to dry over a scrawny tree nearby. I tiptoed over a patch of broken shells to reach the smooth sand, where the dogs' paw prints mixed with the etchings of shorebirds.

"Hey, look at this conch shell." Bonnie held up her sun-bleached prize. "It's in great shape. Need a broken starfish, Mam? There's only one arm missing."

"Don't take it unless it's been dead a long time." Mam was picking through a pocket of smaller shells. "I don't want decaying, smelly sea creatures on the food table."

I rinsed off an olive shell in the water, the sand squeezing between my toes.

Mam saw me and decided I was having too much fun. "Just get shells, I'll wash them later. I'm going up over this dune."

Chloe took off after her. Doc looked at me. "Go on," I said. "Run. Go run with Chloe. Just don't roll on the beach." Wet, sandy dogs are right up there with wet socks. Doc bounded off, the same color as the sea oats waving in the light breeze.

It didn't take Bonnie and me long to fill our buckets. I sat on a driftwood log. Bonnie joined me, holding out her hand. "I haven't seen any sea glass, but I did find two nice shark teeth."

"You've always had a good eye for them."

Uncle James and Daddy had taught us to look for shark teeth before we knew how to ride bikes. Nearsighted even then, I picked up jagged triangles of black shells as often as teeth. Bonnie's jar always held more than mine or Mam's, although my brother, Jack, discovered the biggest shark tooth we ever found—a gray monster the size of a big toe. He wanted to wear it on a thong around his neck until Uncle James told him about the snaggle-toothed shark on the lookout for his lost chopper. "But he'll take a spare ankle if he can find it."

Bonnie stretched her legs and wiggled her toes. "Where's Mam?" I pointed over the dunes behind us. "Margaret Ann, we're through!" she yelled, scaring the sandpipers at the surf's edge.

Mam called from behind us, "Hey, y'all come here! Come see what I found!"

She was standing ankle high in green weeds beside a small clearing. "This looks familiar. I know it's not poison ivy or poison oak, but I can't remember what poison sumac looks like. And I don't want to pick any for the arrangements until I'm sure I know what it is."

I knew what it was. So did Bonnie. "Oh, my word, Mam," she said. "It's dope, you dope."

"Dope?"

"Marijuana," I said. "Pot. Weed. Cannabis. Granville County homegrown. It looks like maybe somebody was smoking out here and a few seeds scattered."

"More than a few," Bonnie said, bypassing a stand of stunted cacti to further examine the plants. "These are stragglers, but this patch back here has been cultivated. Somebody's got themselves a nice little garden."

"They must come by pretty often," I said, crumpling a brown stalk in my hand and holding it to my nose. It smelled like every rock concert I'd ever been to. "There's not any fresh water out here, unless they've put a storage tank up in the woods. That looks like a path over there."

"I don't like the look of this whole setup." Mam surveyed the isolated surroundings. "Let's go on back before whoever decides to come check on their crop."

"Wait, I gotta pee." Bonnie hurried over to some myrtle bushes. "Don't leave me."

"Good grief, hurry up." I didn't want to linger either. Instead of looking like a shady haven, the woods suddenly seemed dark and dangerous. I felt goose bumps on my arms. "Where are the dogs?"

"They went thataway." Mam pointed to the path into the woods. "They're chasing after something." She put two fingers to her mouth and gave an ear-splitting whistle. "Chloe! Doc!"

Barking came from our right. "They're back on the beach now," I said. "Bonnie, come on."

She came tripping up just then, hopping as she zipped her jeans. "Whew, it's snaky and buggy back there. I don't see how those people on reality shows do it. I wouldn't stay out here in this jungle for a million dollars."

"That's why they do it," Mam said. "But I think they want the fame as much as the money. Personally, I could do without the whole world seeing me with bird crap in my hair." She looked up at the flock of gulls bearing down on us like we were handing out potato chips. "Let's vamoose."

I felt better when we trudged back over the dunes to the beach. It was broad daylight now. Doc and Chloe met us, sniffing at our haul before streaking off again, barking their heads off.

"Fool dogs," Mam said. "There's nothing to see."

She was right. The tide had receded, leaving a broad expanse of shell-speckled sand studded here and there with large whelks.

Mam reached down for one. I took off my baseball hat and wiped my forehead. It was getting hot in the sun. We'd been here longer than planned.

Bonnie peered at the beach. "Where's the boat?" she said.

CHAPTER THIRTEEN

Wet and Wired, or What Is a Tussie Mussie?

"Dadgummit!" Mam said. "Someone stole the boat!"

"No, they didn't," I said, my heart dropping. "Look."

The Sea Fox was bobbing in the inlet, heading out to the ocean with the tide. Already, it was almost a football field away, too far to swim.

"Drat!" Mam dropped her bucket and ran to the water's edge. "I thought we had it anchored high enough. The current must be stronger than I thought. J. T.'s gonna kill me if I lose his boat."

"It's not lost yet," Bonnie said. "J. T.'s not going to be happy when you call him on your cell and tell him what happened, but you can be sure he'll come get his boat. We may have to climb a tree to get a signal, though."

Mam's face brightened, then fell. "I left the cell phone on the boat so I wouldn't lose it. And don't look at me like that, Bonnie Lynn. You're the one who pitched the anchor."

"Right where you told me to. I cannot believe you left the cell—"

"Hey!" I interrupted. "Arguing isn't going to get the boat back. We need . . ." I stopped and turned my head. Was that a motor? Bonnie and Mam turned, too. A boat was coming around the side of the island.

"Yoo-hoo!" Mam yelled. "Help! Our boat's floating away!"

Bonnie and I joined in, waving our arms. "Over here! Over here!" The dogs barked frantically.

The small boat cut across the channel a half-mile in front of us, seeming to slow before speeding out to sea. Soon, it was just a yellow speck on the horizon. Then it was gone.

"Maybe they didn't hear us," Mam said forlornly.

"Are you kidding?" Bonnie kicked the sand in front of her. "The way water carries sound, they probably heard us at the Edisto marina. There's no way they didn't hear us."

"Well, why didn't they stop?" Mam was cross now. "Maybe they were almost out of gas. Maybe they've gone to get help."

"I don't think so." I looked up the beach to the cooler. At least we had water. "They didn't want us to see them."

"Why not?"

Bonnie scowled. "Think about it, Mam. They got close enough to recognize our boat but not close enough for us to get a good look at them."

"Oh, you mean because they're the dope fiends? They don't know we know that."

"They can't take that chance," Bonnie said, starting to trudge back up the beach. "I'm going to get something to drink. Did you put the dog bowl in the cooler, or is it on the boat, too?"

"In the cooler," Mam said. "And I stuck some Hershey's bars in there. I thought we might want them."

Bonnie grinned. "Ah, chocolate. The answer to everything."

"Except getting our boat back. J. T. is going to kill me."

"Possibly," I said. "But come get some water and a candy bar. You'll feel better. You know, the condemned always eat a hearty meal. Or at least chocolate."

The dogs slurped water noisily, nudging each other out of the way.

Mam had even stuck some treats in a plastic bag for them. We all sat in the shade, munching.

"Now what?" Mam asked, licking her fingers. "It's not just J. T., you know. We've got all the flowers to do."

"We?" I stretched out on my back and pulled my cap over my eyes. "Where do you get this *we* stuff? I don't know how to make corsages."

"Neither does Bonnie. I'll teach you. Everyone's going to have to help. All hands on deck. But first, we have to get home." She looked behind us. "Maybe we could go through the woods to the other side and then swim across the creek and walk and get help."

"Don't be ridiculous, Mam." Bonnie poked around in the cooler. "That would take forever, and by the time we made it through the woods, the tide would be coming back in, and no way could we swim Drowning Creek. Besides, we'd probably get snake-bit before then."

Mam jumped up. "Well, I'm not going to just sit here and wait for someone to figure out where we are. That could take hours. J. T.'s probably just getting up. Let's spell out *Help* in the sand so a plane will see us."

"From thirty thousand feet?"

Jets followed the coast on their way north and south. Sometimes, you could see contrails and the sun glinting off a tiny speck. And every now and then, we'd hear fighter jets from Parris Island screaming in the distance.

"There's the Coast Guard helicopter," Mam said. "It's over at Johns Island. They're always going out looking for lost boats."

"If they know they're lost." Bonnie settled down beside me.

"We have to be prepared." Mam was going into Girl Scout mode. "I'm going to use this shell to start drawing. Come help."

I groaned and sat up, blinking in the sunlight. I stared at the Sea Fox lolling in the water. "Can't you use your special powers for good instead of evil and just wish us onto the boat?"

"What are you talking about?" Mam struck off down the beach, a big, broken whelk in her hand. She watched *Law & Order* reruns. I preferred *Charmed* and *Buffy the Vampire Slayer*. We should have watched *Survivor*.

I put my head to my knees but looked up when I heard splashing. Were Chloe and Doc going for a swim? No, they were sacked out with me and Bonnie. They both lifted their heads when I did.

"Mam, what are you doing?" I hollered. "You can't go swimming. That's a riptide."

Bonnie sat up. "Good grief, Mam. Stop!"

Mam turned. She was thigh-high in the surf. "Look!" She pointed at the boat. "It's not moving any farther. I think the anchor's stuck on something. And it's pretty shallow now that the tide's out. I probably can walk most of the way."

"Wait!" I sprinted down the beach, Bonnie on my heels. The dogs galloped in front of us. "You don't know how deep it is. There might be a drop-off."

Mam kept going. "Hang onto the dogs. I'm fine."

Chloe barked as Bonnie dragged her back from the water. Doc looked at me, waiting for instructions. "Good dog. Stay here." If I had to go after Mam, I didn't want to worry about him, too. I waded into the water, feeling the tug of the current.

Mam was up to her waist, bobbing on the crest of a wave. "Look, no problem."

Then she disappeared.

"Mam!" I waded farther out. I'd done some lifeguarding as a camp counselor, but that was at a mountain lake. The ocean was altogether different. Even the strongest swimmers could get sucked out by the tide or wiped out by a wave. "Mam!"

Bonnie screamed, "Mam, where are you?"

I saw Mam's head break the surface. "There she is!" She was now closer to the boat than to us, breast-stroking toward her goal.

"Oh, geez, she's going to get swept past it." Bonnie struggled to hold Chloe, who had pulled her into the water. "Dear Lord, please help Margaret Ann. No, Chloe. You stay with us." Bonnie was on her backside, gripping the dog's collar. "Do you see her?"

"Yes. She's almost there." I held my breath, willing Mam to reach the boat. I saw her arms flail. "Come on, Mam! You can do it!"

Chloe and Bonnie were beside me now. Doc jumped into the water, thinking it was a game. I lunged for his collar. There was salt in my eyes—either tears or ocean. I couldn't see. Where was Mam?

"Look!" Bonnie yelled. "She's hanging onto the side of the boat! I'm not sure she can get up."

"Hang on and rest a minute!" I called. I could see Mam trying to work her foot up the side of the boat. It flopped back in the water. If she could just get some leverage, she'd be able to throw herself over the side. She hung by both arms for a minute, then started inching her way toward the stern.

"She's going for the propeller!" Bonnie cried.

"Smart girl! Look, she's up. She's in!"

"Oh, thank God." Bonnie and I watched as Mam stood and waved weakly in triumph. She grabbed the taut anchor line and gave it a yank. The boat moved, and Mam waved again. Then she tried putting her hand into the wet pocket of her clinging khakis. Bonnie looked dismayed. "If she doesn't have the key, I'm going to kill her."

⌒)

"Where's the glue gun?" Bonnie asked.

"You won't need it, since I wire everything," explained Mam as she set us up to make corsages.

Our trip back had been uneventful, although we had one bad moment when J. T. hailed us from the dock. "Have a good trip?" he'd asked, extending his hand to Mam. She'd grabbed it and then surprised him with a big hug once she was on the dock.

"I thought you were going to Columbia," she said. "I didn't expect to see you."

"My meeting got postponed till next week. You look like you've been swimming."

Mam grinned. "Oh, the dogs knocked me in. I gotta take a shower before I freeze my butt off."

"I'll give the dogs a bath," I'd said, figuring that would postpone any flower fixings.

But I hadn't counted on J. T. "I'll do it," he said. "And I'll clean the boat, too." He winked at Bonnie and me over Mam's shoulder. "Margaret Ann, I know you need the girls' help with the flowers."

Bonnie had given him the same evil look she now directed at the floral paraphernalia in front of her.

Mam stood over us. "You *can* use floral glue, Cissy, to seal these roses after Lindsey cuts them. Be sure to put them on paper towels." She turned to me with a bunch of purple-blue roses and showed me where she'd sliced the stem of one. "About an inch down, Lindsey, and then pass them on to Cissy. Cut twenty-one." *Cut twenty-one.* It sounded like a poker game. "That should cover the corsages for mothers, grand-mothers, the soloist, and the director," Mam continued. "No, wait, add eight, no nine boutonnieres for the groomsmen. I always do one extra. You know how guys can clown around and break one. That makes thirty."

"Thirty," I repeated, then promptly pricked my finger on a thorn. "Ouch!"

"Sorry," Mam said, not sounding sorry at all. "I didn't strip these, as we're just cutting off the heads."

" 'Off with their heads,' " I muttered, thinking again of *Alice in Won-derland*. First, Mam had been like the White Rabbit, complaining about our lateness. Now, she was the Red Queen.

"Oops! I forgot that the moms are carrying tussie mussies, so sub-tract six, and that makes twenty-four. Got it? I'll add some Sweetheart roses, too, and all these leaves that Bonnie's gonna wire. Why are y'all looking so confused?"

"Is a tussie mussie one of those little bouquets in a cone?" I thought it sounded like the nonsense words Lewis Carroll made up in "Jabberwocky."

"Stop grumbling, Lindsey. And why are you frowning, Bonnie? I'm going to feed you."

"I'm staying here, you know." Bonnie looked at the floral wire with bemusement. "You'd be feeding me anyway."

Mam ignored her, cutting the wire in thirds and showing us how to bend it to look like one of Nanny's hairpins. Then she demonstrated weaving the wire in an ivy leaf ("It's kind of like sewing") and twisting the floral tape around the wire in a downward stretching motion. As she turned away to the sink, I watched Bonnie mess the first one up and sit on it. One less ivy leaf. Her look dared me to say anything.

I finished the roses and handed them off to Cissy. I hoped Mam didn't notice I was free. Where was MaryMar, anyway? How had she escaped our craft prison? Since she was the reason we were in jail, she ought to be in here helping. I looked behind me at the doorway to the den. I could hear the TV.

"She's watching *Steel Magnolias*," Bonnie whispered. "Let's leave her be."

Mam saw me turn my head. "Good, Lindsey. Now, I'll show you how to make a corsage bow." She reached for her file and pulled out a typed sheet. "Let's see. We only need four bows. Use this lavender ribbon." She started fashioning a bow, making sure I was watching. "I've never made a bow this color for a wedding corsage, but you know Beth. She wants everything to match. This was as close to Pinckney purple as I could come. At least it's sheer and goes well with the Bluebird roses. The Sweethearts are ivory, so that will tone it down some." She finished the bow and wired it. "Nice and tight, okay, Lindsey?"

I didn't think that was really a question, so I just picked up the ribbon and scissors. In real jail, we wouldn't get sharp objects.

Mam saw Bonnie clumsily twisting the leaves. "Here, I'll help you. I use at least five leaves per corsage and two per boutonniere."

"We need thirty-seven leaves, Aunt Bonnie," Cissy piped up proudly.

"Gee, thanks for the math lesson." Bonnie waited until Mam wasn't looking to slide another messed-up leaf under her backside. "Why don't you bend this wire for me, Cissy?"

Twenty-five minutes later, I finished my first bow. In the same amount of time, Mam had soaked oasis for fifteen containers and secured them all with thick green tape. All the while, she lectured us on how we'd hide the tape and the containers with greenery after we finished the corsages. I eyed the bags of kudzu and pittosporum by the sink.

"We'll move under the house for that," said Mam. "It's too messy for the kitchen, at least if you want to eat here. I have leftover backbone and rice, butter beans, and macaroni and cheese."

"What's for dessert?" asked Bonnie.

Anticipating the question, Mam held up a brownie mix from the lower cabinet.

"That'll work," said Bonnie, jumping from her stool and snatching the box from Mam. "I'll make them. Here, Cissy, only twenty-nine more leaves to go."

"Aunt Bonnie!" Cissy play-pouted. If her breakup with Jimmy was bothering her, you couldn't tell it. "I need to buy something awesome for the wedding. I'm supposed to be set up with this freshman from Clemson, one of the groomsmen. He even knows how to shag, and I've got to look real cute on the dance floor."

"What's his name?" My second bow looked like something Peaches had played with. Where had that extra loop come from?

"I don't remember his name, but I think it starts with a B." Cissy was deftly twisting wire and leaves. "Can I go into Charleston tomorrow with Ashley to shop? I've got enough gas in the Honda, but do you think Daddy will advance me some money till I get my Pinckney paycheck? Maybe you could ask him for me."

Being an only child, Cissy could twist J. T. around her little finger, but she liked her mother to soften him up first. He was as protective of her as our daddies had been with us—although not as embarrassing. In high school, Uncle James met Mam's dates at the door with comments like, "Don't you have any shoes, boy?" J. T. figured that any boy who could survive Mam's interrogations on immediate plans, future intentions, and family connections didn't need to be further terrorized. His easygoing manner was a natural foil to Mam's hyperactivity.

Which was why even she was stunned into silence when J. T. suddenly came crashing up the stairs. "Margaret Ann!" he hollered, his face red. "You want to explain to me what this was doing in my boat?" He held out what was undeniably a stalk of marijuana.

Mam, Bonnie, and I looked at each other guiltily. We were busted.

It was Cissy who spoke up. "Oh, Daddy, what's the big deal? It's just Pinckney Plant."

CHAPTER FOURTEEN

Gone to Pot

"Pinckney Plant?" J. T. bellowed, his face turning even redder. "What the devil is Pinckney Plant?"

"Well, that's what Marietta calls it," Cissy said defensively.

"Marietta?" Mam was as puzzled as the rest of us. "What does Marietta have to do with this?"

"She grows Pinckney Plant in her herb garden. You've seen it, Aunt Lindsey."

"I have?" Everybody was looking at me now. "Marietta's got some mint and rosemary in that little plot by the stable. Posey fenced it so the deer can't get to it. But I don't remember seeing any, um, Pinckney Plant. Are you sure you're not mixing it up with something else? Lettuce-leaf basil, or maybe cherry tomatoes?"

"The leaves are similar." Bonnie took the stalk from J. T., who had gone from boil to simmer. "But I've never heard it called Pinckney Plant." She grinned. "Who knew? Reefer madness on Indigo."

"Reefer madness?" Cissy's voice shot up an octave. "You mean it's pot? Daddy, honest, I didn't know. Marietta said it was Pinckney Plant. Mama, tell him. You have to believe me. I don't do drugs."

J. T. patted Cissy on the shoulder, upset that he had upset her. "It's all right, Cissy. Don't cry. I believe you. We'll get this straightened out." He shook his head. "I still don't see how this got in the boat, though."

"It's mine," Bonnie volunteered, daring Mam or me to say anything. "I found it on Lost Beach and stuck it in with my shells. I was going to tell Will about it when he came over. I thought he might want to check it out. I just forgot because we had to do the flowers."

Mam nodded vigorously. "It must have fallen out of your tote bag. We were in such a hurry there at the end, slinging everything in. I tell you, I was so worn out swimming after the boat that—"

"You went swimming after the boat?" J. T.'s face started to redden again. "When? Where? Margaret Ann, what haven't you told me? I think you better start at the beginning."

"I always cry at the end." MaryMar rubbed her eyes and sniffed. The *Steel Magnolias* credits were rolling on the TV in the den. "It's just so sad about Shelby, her collapsing like that after her mama gave her her kidney."

"Mmm," I said absently, picking up a copy of *Southern Living* off the coffee table. A cover line advised, "Make the Most of Your Herb Garden." Maybe they should talk to Marietta. Will would certainly want to, once he heard about Pinckney Plant. J. T. was on the phone with him right now. I expected he'd be over shortly to give us what-for, although J. T. had done a pretty fair job once he sent Cissy to her room. Even Mam hadn't tried to interrupt him. Now, she was fixing dinner, Bonnie was setting the table, and I'd just finished carrying the centerpiece containers downstairs.

MaryMar continued to chat about how much she loved Julia Roberts. "She is just my most favorite actress. I would love to be her, not that I would ever want twins." She shuddered. "I wonder if they run in her family. They do in mine."

That got my attention. "MaryMar, don't you have family on Indigo? How come you weren't staying with them for the wedding?" Or
now, for that matter.

"I'm not an Indigo Futch," MaryMar said indignantly. "The name is
just coincidence. I asked my daddy about it one time when I was little,
and he said, 'Those Futches are a different breed of dog.' He's one of
the Florida Futches. They're a real important family down there."

If you go by numbers and reputation, the Futches are a force on
Indigo. They and the Smoaks are the island equivalents of the Hatfields
and McCoys, alternately feuding and intermarrying. And they are certainly well known to local law enforcement and social workers for raising Cain—and babies—on the north end of the island.

"I don't look anything like the Futches from here," MaryMar continued, flipping her hair over her shoulder. That was true. No Indigo
Futch had ever entered a beauty pageant, to put it kindly. "And if you
must know, my parents and sister live in Jacksonville now. She has
twins." She made it sound like a rash. "Actually, my mother is related
to the Seabrooks." It's a Low Country joke that everyone claims to be
related to the Seabrooks. The Pinckneys come a close second in the
race for prominent kinfolk. "And one of my great-aunts was a Pinckney."
MaryMar smiled demurely. "Miss Augusta has always taken a special
interest in me."

The phone rang, and I picked it up, only to hear Miss Augusta
already talking to Mam. My cousin has some sort of telepathic connection with BellSouth.

"Is Lindsey there?" Miss Augusta cut off Mam. "I want to speak to
her."

"Hello, Miss Augusta. How are you?"

"I've already told Margaret Ann I'm as well as can be expected.
You can hang up now, dear. I'm talking to Lindsey. I know how busy
you are."

I heard the click. A moment later, Mam was standing in the doorway listening in while I listened to Miss Augusta saying she'd been
trying to reach me all day.

"I've been helping Mam with the flowers for the wedding," I said, knowing it was no use reminding her that Thursday was my day off. As far as Miss Augusta was concerned, I was always on duty as her stand-in. And once she returned from Bayview, no doubt Posey and I would take turns as chauffeur—shades of *Driving Miss Daisy*.

"Oh, yes, the wedding," Miss Augusta said. "I'm sure it will be a very nice affair, although why young people don't get married in a church anymore is beyond me. And speaking of church, you did take care of the Easter lilies, didn't you?"

"Yes, ma'am." I'd told her this at least twice already. "For both the church and the plantation cemetery."

"I hope they're better looking than these here at Bayview. Really, I'm going to have to speak to them about it. Also, the meal service. I believe their green beans are out of a can."

"That's too bad." I tried to sound sympathetic. Surely, she hadn't called just to complain about vegetables.

"Actually, Lindsey"—Miss Augusta lowered her voice—"I was hoping you might have some news. Is it true that poor Spivey girl is still in the hospital and not able to talk?"

"That's my understanding." So she didn't know Lorna was dead. That meant the sheriff's department was still keeping a lid on events.

"And MaryMar has gone into hiding because she's afraid for her life?"

"I've heard that, too," I said, looking at the object of our conversation, who was pretending not to listen while thumbing through a *TV Guide*. Mam was impatiently snapping a dishtowel.

"Well, I believe I know where she is." Miss Augusta sounded pleased with herself.

"Really?"

"Yes. Maudie's daughter-in-law is friends with Carol Beckwith in Charleston, who knows Ron and Elise Simmons. And Carol says Elise is getting ready to serve papers on Ron because of MaryMar. I am very disappointed in MaryMar for becoming involved with a married man, although I never much cared for Elise. She was an Irving, of course, and no better than she should be." Miss Augusta sniffed. "But that's no never mind. Elise found out because she was at Skatell's Jewelry in

Charleston on Monday and discovered Ron had bought something for MaryMar. And she told Carol she was sure the two of them had been at the Indigo house. Ron is supposedly away on a business trip. I think MaryMar must be with him."

"Oh." I didn't know what else to say.

Miss Augusta did. "Normally, I wouldn't stoop to such gossip, but since this is a matter of some urgency, I thought it best to contact the authorities. But Will hasn't returned my call yet, so I want you to have him call me."

"Me?" I saw Mam frowning. She obviously thought I wasn't holding up my end of the conversation.

Miss Augusta was brisk. "Now, Lindsey, don't be coy. I may be an old woman, but I know when a man takes a special interest in a woman, and when that interest is returned. You two have been very discreet, I must say, and that is admirable. And I will continue to respect your privacy, but I think it's important that Will has this information as soon as possible." She paused.

"Yes, ma'am. As soon as possible."

I heard a sigh of satisfaction. "Excellent. I will expect his call. Of course, it's possible he already has reached this conclusion. Carol says Elise says Will was at Skatell's the same time as her on Monday." Her voice suddenly dropped. "Someone is at my door. Good-bye."

I listened to dead air a moment before turning off the phone and handing it to Mam. Will had told me he needed to go to Skatell's to get his watch fixed. When it came to wild rumors, MaryMar and I were in the same boat.

"Now, tell me again about this other boat you saw." At Mam's insistence, Will had gathered with us around her work table under the house so the centerpieces could get finished before midnight. "Bonnie, you said maybe it was a Key West. What color yellow?"

"Banana cream pudding," Bonnie said promptly.

"Maybe more like Lady Banksia roses," added Mam.

"Light yellow," I said. I could see Will's jaw tightening, although he had been remarkably patient in extracting our account of the island adventure. "Black motor."

The others nodded.

"Yamaha? Evinrude? Mercury?" Will prodded.

"It was too far away to tell," Bonnie said.

I nodded. Unless it was spelled out in large letters, I wouldn't know the difference.

"Just one person?" Will asked.

"I think so," Mam said. "But there could have been somebody crouched down." She added some greenery to one of the centerpieces and gave it a considering look. "What do y'all think?"

"About the centerpiece or the boat?" Bonnie sounded slightly irked. "Pay attention, Mam. This is serious stuff."

"I'm happy at least one of you is taking it seriously." Will looked straight at me.

Really, that wasn't fair. Lost Beach hadn't been my idea. And Will hadn't said we needed to stay at the house with MaryMar. The latter wasn't in on our discussion. Will had brought her luggage from Centerville, at which point she'd gone into ecstasy, escaping to Cissy's room to discard my jeans and T-shirt for presumably more attractive attire.

"It was just one person, as far as we could tell," I said to Will. "It looked like a guy."

"Humph. Well, you haven't given me much to go on. If a boat's not white around here, it's likely yellow. And with it being spring break, there are boats all over." Will closed his notebook.

"What now?" Bonnie asked, eager for any diversion from the floral arts.

"I go do my job, and y'all stay here and don't talk about any of this with anyone." He stood. "Please." Mam might have said something, but she was too intent on her arrangement. And were those floral pins in her mouth? "Lindsey, walk me out, please. There's something I need to ask you about Miss Augusta." He smiled at the others. "Night, Mam, Bonnie. Thanks for the brownie." He paused. "I trust you didn't add any Pinckney Plant."

The man knew a good exit line.

The marsh smelled pungent in the damp night air. A few stars peeked through streaky clouds.

"So," Will said, leaning against the driver's door of his SUV, "what did you tell the cousins about Miss Augusta's call?"

"Just that she wanted to talk to you." I leaned next to him so our shoulders were touching. Well, not quite. My shoulder hits him mid-biceps, which means my head rests nicely under his chin, given the opportunity. "MaryMar was right there, so I didn't want to go into the stuff about Ron and Elise. Although if Carol Beckwith knows, it'll be all over the Low Country by midnight."

"It's just as well. Let people think MaryMar is with Ron. I'm sure she would be if she had her druthers."

"What about Lorna?" I asked.

"What about her?"

"How long are you going to keep it a secret that the poor girl is dead?"

"As long as necessary."

I shivered. "It seems so callous doing all this wedding stuff. MaryMar still thinks you're going to let her be a bridesmaid."

"Yeah, I know." He started to say something else but didn't.

"Can I tell Mam and Bonnie about Elise? Mam knows you called Miss Augusta. She'll shoot me if she finds out I knew and didn't tell her."

Will turned toward me. "There are other things you don't tell her."

"That's different. That's us. It's private." I let him kiss me. "But I think people know. Miss Augusta sort of hinted."

"Mmm." Will nuzzled my neck. "We're lucky we've kept it quiet this long." He drew back. "Does it bother you?"

"No, not really. It would probably be easier not having to pretend we just keep running into each other everywhere. Mam basically told MaryMar to keep her girl paws off you, that we're an item."

Will sighed. "Lindsey, we have to talk."

My heart did this elevator-like plunge toward my stomach. In my experience, we-have-to-talk talk is usually bad news. I stepped back. "What about?"

"Something I've been meaning to tell you since I got back, but there hasn't been a chance. And I didn't want to."

The bad news was becoming worse. "What?"

"I'm going away for a while."

"Where?" I said stupidly. "For how long?"

"That's the thing," he said. "I can't tell you. I'm not even sure myself. I'm going to be part of this new coastal drug-enforcement team that's made up of federal, state, and local forces. It'll probably be somewhere on the Carolina coast, or maybe Georgia. Otherwise, they wouldn't have tapped me. But it's a temporary assignment—four months probably, six at the outside."

"Oh," I said, processing the news. I'd recently turned my life upside down on account of Will—well, mostly on his account—and now here he was riding off into the sunset to fight the war on drugs. "Will it involve operations like Lost Beach?"

"We already knew about that. We've had our eye on that plot for a while."

"Do you know whose it is?"

"I can't tell you, you know that," he said. "And you know you can't discuss this with the cousins either."

"I know." I looked at the ground. J. T. needed some more oyster shells for the drive. "When are you going?"

"Not for a couple weeks. I have to clear up this investigation here." Will tipped my chin up. "So?"

I tried to smile. "Absence makes the heart grow fonder." I sure hoped so. Long-distance relationships took a lot of work. Heck, any relationship was work. But Will and I had been separated for years and were still new at being together again. I was afraid that with Will gone, my old insecurities about his long-ago betrayal would resurface. I'd let MaryMar get to me for no real reason. I needed to trust Will. "I'll miss you," I said.

"And I'll miss you. Meanwhile, though, you and Mam and Bonnie need to stop charging into these situations you don't know anything about."

I jerked my head up. "You wouldn't know about Pinckney Plant if it wasn't for us."

"That's another kettle of fish." Will shook his head. "I'll talk to Marietta. There's no need for you to worry about it."

"What do you mean?"

"Just that I'll take care of it."

"Will, I need to know what's going on at Pinckney. I'm the acting manager."

"Which means you should cooperate with local law enforcement." Will looked bemused. "I don't see the problem. It's just that I worry."

"Well, don't." I hoped he didn't see the tears welling in my eyes. I always cry when I get mad. He'd probably think it was because he was going away. "I can take care of myself. I did a pretty good job of it the last twenty years, thank you very much. Give me some credit."

"I do. Lindsey, let's not fight. We're both tired. You've got a lot on your plate right now."

I shrugged off his arm. "It's nothing I can't handle. And if you think a couple of kisses are going to turn me into some little girly-poo without a mind of her own, then you've got another thing coming, buster. Pinckney Plant is my business. So put that in your pipe and smoke it."

I knew a good exit line, too.

CHAPTER FIFTEEN

Picture This, or Diamond Hopefuls

Morning fog blanketed the marsh, wisps of smoky mist drifting across the blacktop. I drove carefully toward Middle House, peering through the windshield. The defroster was on, but I'd also rolled down a back window so Doc could poke his nose out. Peaches looked like a sitting hen in his carrier in the front seat next to me. He was going to miss watching those stupid goldfish in the tank in Mam's den.

"You better count 'em," I'd told her as I packed my stuff. "What are you planning to do with them after the wedding, anyway?"

"Donate them to Bayview," she'd replied absently as she continued preparing the fragile orchids for the groomsmen's leis. "Beth's going to take some of the flowers from the reception home and send others to the hospital. We'll have to carry the palm trees back to the church in time for the Easter service."

Bonnie looked up from her coffee. "Don't you just love the *we*?"

She sighed, annoyed that I was breaking loose from our floral prison.

"Pinckney calls." I hoisted my duffel bag and the cat carrier. Peaches was the heavier. "Y'all have fun. I'll see you this afternoon after the bridesmaids' luncheon. Perk up, Bonnie. The food will be good. BoBo's is catering. They're worth the drive to Edisto."

"Edisto?" She set down her coffee cup and looked accusingly at Mam. "The luncheon's there? You didn't tell me that *we*"—she emphasized the pronoun—"have to deliver centerpieces all the way over there."

Mam frowned at an orchid smaller than the rest. "You don't have to go. You can stay here with MaryMar. I think she's going to watch *Steel Magnolias* again."

I'd left them bickering. I had my own problems. As soon as I dropped off Doc and Peaches, I needed to go to Pinckney and talk with Posey about security. I wasn't sure whether to tackle him or Marietta first about Pinckney Plant. You couldn't tell me a man who knew the scientific name of every palm on the plantation hadn't recognized marijuana when he fenced in Marietta's garden. On the other hand, maybe it wasn't dope that Cissy had seen, but some look-alike herb. Maybe I ought to start with Marietta. But I needed to ask somebody, Will's orders to the contrary. Part of me felt guilty about my hissy fit the night before. After all, it was good that Will cared enough about me to worry. But I had every right to be in the loop where the plantation was concerned. If only he hadn't been so condescending.

"Will thinks I'm some sort of fragile flower," I told Doc and Peaches. "Humph! Step on this magnolia blossom and you'll break your foot."

I braked going around the curve near Crab Creek. The fog was starting to break up in spots. Sunlight glinted off the Bottle Tree. The Indigo landmark was a bare, lone tree in the middle of the marsh. No one knew for certain who kept it decorated with colored glass bottles and bright ribbons. But it was ready for Easter, with yellow and pink streamers. At Christmas, they were green and red.

Red.

I saw it as I came out of the curve. It looked like . . . No, it couldn't be. I braked. Doc staggered behind me, trying to stay upright as I pulled the CR-V to the shoulder. I turned on my safety lights and got out.

A red car was half submerged in the marsh. Cissy? Omigod. Then I remembered that her Honda was parked at Mam's, and that she was still asleep.

Who, then?

Wheel tracks indicated where the car had come round the curve and plowed off the road. And judging by the soggy imprints and crushed vegetation, it hadn't been long ago. As for who, red cars were as ubiquitous as black pickups.

"Anyone out there?" I yelled. "Are you okay?" There was no answer. Doc whined, thrusting his gold snout through the rear window. "Good boy," I said, petting him for comfort. "You stay here."

There was no use trying my cell phone. Even if I climbed on the roof of the CR-V, I wouldn't get a signal in this, the lowest of low spots. But I couldn't just leave and go for help if somebody might still be in the car, maybe hurt.

Okay, I needed new work boots anyway. It was time for this magnolia blossom to show her stuff. When I gingerly stepped off the shoulder, my right foot immediately sank in the pluff mud. Yuck. Gnats swarmed my head. I waved them off as I trekked toward the car. Was that a figure slumped over the steering wheel?

A horn sounded. Doc barked. I turned to see a giant palmetto bug seemingly suspended in midair. It was Lonnie in his white van.

"What happened?" He was halfway out his door, but I waved him back.

"Go for help." I pointed across the bridge. "The Murrays have a phone. First drive on the left, after about a mile. Or go to the landing. Somebody will be there for sure. Call the sheriff."

"I'll come out there," Lonnie said. "You come on back."

"No!" Why did guys have to be so macho? "It'll be quicker if you go. Go on!"

He went. I turned back toward the red car, which seemed to have settled more deeply in the muck and spartina. Oh, please, let help get here quickly. Maybe I should have let Lonnie take over, but it was too late now.

The mud sucked at my boots. The car's trunk was facing toward me, the license plate hidden by reeds. The sun bouncing off the rearview mirror hit me straight in the eye. I blinked. Hallelujah! The driver's door was partway open. Maybe whoever it was had gotten out. I looked around quickly. Heaven help me if they were lying in the marsh.

I looked up at the sound of a siren. Lonnie must have gone the faster route, to the landing. Will swung the gold-and-white SUV across the road so it was parked crossways. Behind him were Lonnie and Mike.

"There's no one in the car." Holding onto the door, I could see the interior was empty. But the windshield was smashed, and there was either mud or, geez, blood spattered on the steering wheel and front seat. My knees went weak, and my stomach started to come up my throat. Get a grip, I told myself, clutching the door harder. Maybe if I leaned in and opened the glove compartment . . .

"Don't get in!" Will tromped through the mud. "It might sink more. Are you all right?"

"I'm fine, but I don't know about whoever. I think there's blood." I closed my eyes.

"Here, now." Will steadied my shoulder and gently detached me from the car door, handing me off to Lonnie. "Help her back to the road, please. Mike, circle around the other side and let's see if we see anybody."

I let go of Lonnie's sturdy forearm and stood up straight. "I can make it back myself. Let Lonnie help."

Lonnie gave me a grateful look. He was dying to get in on the action. "I'll go over this way toward the woods."

I stepped backwards and almost tripped. A white leatherette album was lying face up on a hummock of grass. It must have been slung from the car. It hadn't been in the marsh long. "Our Wedding" gleamed in gold calligraphy on the cover. I shook a few drops of water off the spine and opened it. It contained photograph after photograph, most in color but some in black-and-white.

"Will," I said to his back. He was doing exactly what he'd told me not to do, leaning across the front seat to open the glove compartment. "Will, I think you'll want to see this."

"Just a minute." He reappeared holding an amber prescription bottle and the car's registration papers. He looked at the label on the plastic container and quickly shook open the registration. "The car belongs to—"

"Scott Russo," I interjected, holding out the photo album. "Look at this."

Will frowned at me. "I know he's a photographer, Lindsey."

"He's also a stalker."

"What?"

"All these pictures . . . ," I said, swallowing hard. "They're all of MaryMar."

"Scott the photographer is MaryMar's stalker!" Mam burst into the kitchen at Pinckney like a Boykin puppy chasing squirrels. "I tried to call you from Edisto to see if you'd heard, but Marietta said you weren't here."

I looked at the clock. It was almost two. She must have flown to get here so fast from the bridesmaids' luncheon. It didn't surprise me that she knew the headline. Miss Augusta had already called to confirm the rumors circulating at Bayview.

"I was helping look for Scott," I told Mam, swallowing some Coke. I couldn't wait to tell her the next part. "I found"—I chewed some ice, relishing the moment—"his car and the evidence."

"You did? Oh, I want to know everything. Wait." She went to the back door. "Bonnie, hurry up! Lindsey knows stuff." Her face was eager.

"Shh! Don't shout. There's a tour in the parlor," I said.

"No, they're already outside, or maybe that's the next group waiting. You'd think we had enough to do today without giving tours."

What was this *we* thing? She wasn't the one who had to worry about keeping the plantation open before and after the Chesnut wedding. Easter weekend and spring break were bringing out the crowds, even though the weather today was uncooperative. It hadn't rained yet, but the sky was cloudy.

"The island's under a tornado watch," Bonnie announced, hefting a bag onto the kitchen table. "Severe thunderstorms, too."

Mam shook her head. "I hope Beth doesn't hear that. She's already in a tizzy over the lunch today and the rehearsal party tonight. She's bound to call and ask me what to do, like I can call the Weather Channel and say, 'Please don't let it rain.' Hurry up and tell us about Scott before the phone rings."

I recounted the morning's events. Mam kept interrupting me— "Which curve?" and "How foggy was it?"—and Bonnie kept shushing her, telling her to let me finish. But it was Bonnie who asked now about the photos.

"It was weird," I said. "At first, I thought they were pictures at someone's wedding, because it was a party scene, and MaryMar had on this long dress. But then I saw her outside in the parking lot at a Wal-Mart, and then in the drive-up line at Chick-fil-A, and you could tell she didn't know she was having her picture taken, especially the Wal-Mart one. She was putting stuff in her convertible, and her coat was hiked up, and there were visible panty lines."

"I declare!" Mam echoed our grandmother's favorite exclamation. "If that doesn't beat all! What happened next?"

"We started looking for Scott 'cause we didn't know if he was lying somewhere hurt or dead. Will called for reinforcements from the fire department, and they were getting ready to organize a grid search when Turner drove up." I paused long enough to gulp some Coke, which was long enough for Mam to start in on the questions again.

"Where were you? What did Will say? What was in the pill bottle?"

"Xanax," I said, holding up my hand in front of Mam's mouth. "Wait! That's not the best part. Scott was sitting in the front seat of Turner's truck, fit as a fiddle except for a cut on his forehead. I was walking Doc by then, right there, so I heard everything. Turner said he'd picked up Scott walking toward the filling station. Scott told him someone shot out his tire and he'd gone into the marsh."

Mam's and Bonnie's words tumbled out on top of each other. "Someone shot at Scott?" "Scott got shot at?"

"So he says." I took a last sip of Coke. I needed to lay off the caffeine until I ate something. "The tow truck from impound was just getting there when I left. I had to change and get here, and Will was leaving anyway, to take Scott to Centerville."

"Did Will arrest him?" Mam wanted to know.

"Not there. Will had the photo album, though. When Scott saw it, he looked more like Peter Rabbit than ever, and Will was Mr. McGregor coming after him with a rake."

"Did Scott say anything?" Bonnie said. "Did he ask for a lawyer?"

"Nope. But y'all are gonna love this. He did ask if he could call his therapist."

Mam hung up the phone. "That woman is going to need serious therapy when this is all over."

"If she's not already in the hollerin' house." Bonnie handed me some finger sandwiches left over from the luncheon. "Who knew being the mother of the bride could be so stressful? I'm glad I've got boys."

"MOGs have their own problems." Mam translated. "Mothers of the grooms. It's awful when the MOG doesn't like the MOB—mother of the bride—or vice versa. Beth and Sunny get on pretty well."

"Wiley's mother is named Sunny?" The cucumber sandwich was divine. Now for the chicken salad.

"I know, isn't that a hoot?" Mam was looking at her list. She crossed out a line. "Her name is Sunny Day!"

"At least she married into the name." Bonnie snorted. "I think parents are just asking for trouble when they name their kids Phil Fuller or Candy Apple."

"You love that your monogram is BLT," I noted. "I wonder what Sunny's maiden name was. She might have kept it."

"Naw," Mam said. "It was Zoellercoffer. Nobody could spell it, and it was at the end of the alphabet. Now, Sue Beth Chesnut's going to be Sue Beth Day. Too many single syllables, if you ask me, which is about the only thing they haven't. But this wedding is going to be good for business. Only one of the bridesmaids is married already, although several of them are diamond hopeful."

"So there's going to be a scramble for the bouquet." Bonnie offered me another sandwich. "You'll have to hustle, Lindsey."

"Very funny." Will and I had sort of made up in the marsh. He hadn't ordered me to go home, and he'd thanked me for my help. But we still had issues, including his impending departure.

Mam didn't even look up. "No, that's all taken care of. Brook's going to catch it. Her boyfriend gave her a ring at Christmas."

"Which one's Brook?" Bonnie asked. "They all look alike to me."

"She's the one who looks like Snow White. I can't keep them straight either, 'cause about half of them are named Kathryn with a *K* or Catherine with a *C* or some variation. There's Kat and Anna Kate and Cathleen, although I always want to call her Pocahontas because she has that long braid."

First Snow White, now Pocahontas. Geez. And Cathleen sounded lovely. "I've always liked that name," I said.

"What, Pocahontas?" Mam crossed another line off her checklist.

"No, silly, Cathleen." My cousin could be remarkably obtuse. Then again, she was preoccupied with wedding preparations. Tonight's rehearsal dinner was small—only fifty people or so, compared with tomorrow's three hundred—but Mam was a control freak. And MOB Beth—down to her last nerve and at her daughter's throat—wasn't helping.

Mam seemed to read my mind. "Beth needs to take a chill pill. You'd have thought it was the end of the world today when she locked her keys in the car."

"You didn't tell me that."

"You were too busy telling us about Scott." Right, put it back on me. "Beth called me just as I drove over the bridge at Edisto. She locked her keys in the car, along with the pearls Sue Beth gave her especially for this weekend. Sunny's already given Sue Beth a pearl necklace and earrings that have been in the Day family forever to wear in the wedding. Since Sue Beth had pearl earrings that were her grandmother's, she gave those to her mama to wear and then used some of her antique-table money to give her mom a necklace to match. She should have, for all the grief Beth keeps getting about the wedding. Sue Beth may look sweet, but she can be stubborn as a mule. She's a princess bride in disguise."

All this came out in a rush, but Bonnie and I were used to Mam's cascading conversations, so we followed it pretty well. The hard part was when she hopscotched from one subject to the next without a break.

"Are there any silver bells, Bonnie?" she said now.

Silver bells are what Mama and Aunt Boodie call Hershey's Kisses. They stash them in a kitchen drawer, and I swear they count them at night to see if we've snuck any. Bonnie leaned back in her chair and opened the drawer where I kept my bag. She tossed six on the table, and we each reached for one.

Mam continued to talk as she unwrapped the candy. "So there's Beth moaning, 'And me without my pearls,' and I told her"—she popped a chocolate into her mouth—"'I'd wait on de yocksmith, since the guys were playing yolf." She was sucking on the candy to make it last longer. "I, um, got the pearls to the uncheon jus as dey were tarthing to eat." She finally paused to swallow.

I slapped my hand on hers as she reached for her second Kiss. "Wait. Finish and then eat, so I don't have to listen so hard."

"Okay, but don't eat mine." She eyed her remaining Kiss like a cat guarding a lizard.

"Mam!"

"Okay, okay. Well, let's see. I was helping Beth put the necklace on in one of the bedrooms at this house near Peter's Point—I would love a house like that—and Beth just sat right down on the bed and started crying silently. Have you ever seen anyone do that? Not a sound, tears rolling down her face. It was scary. I thought she was having a nervous breakdown." Mam looked at Bonnie for confirmation. Bonnie nodded but didn't try to talk with chocolate in her mouth. "We just sat down on the bed on either side of her and patted her on the shoulder.

Finally, she started muttering that the flower girl fell down this morning and knocked out her front tooth. Bonnie told her she bet the flower girl—bless her heart—would look just adorable in the pictures, and Beth said, very calmly, 'What pictures? The wedding photographer has been arrested.' That's how we found out about Scott, only she got it wrong about him being arrested."

"He might be by now," I said. "Poor Beth. What happened then?"

"I told her at least he wasn't a nudie photographer," Mam said. "One of my brides picked out her photographer over the Internet, and it turned out he was into porn."

Bonnie had finished her Kiss. "Beth said, 'And mine is a stalker.' We didn't have the heart to tell her he's a murderer, too. She'd only vaguely heard about Lorna. She's about the only person on Indigo who wasn't at the Gatortorium party."

" 'Cause she was meeting with the cake lady." Mam was hurrying now, eager to get through her story so I'd let her at the chocolate. "I guess MaryMar will get to be in the wedding after all. What do you think?"

"I don't know. Maybe I can call Olivia and see if she knows. I don't call Will when he's on duty, or he'll think I'm in trouble." I moved my hand, and the cousins dived for the chocolate. "What is Beth going to do about a photographer?"

"That's next on my list." Mam's Kiss disappeared into her mouth. She garbled something about calling one of Cissy's friends who was the local stringer for high-school football games.

"I've got a better idea." I picked up the phone. "Olivia Washington, please . . . Hey, it's Lindsey. Listen, I need your help. I know you're off tomorrow, but we're in desperate need of a photographer for this wedding. . . . Oh, come on. I'll let you have my Chico's coupons, and Mam will do the flowers for your next special event." Mam vigorously nodded her assent. "And the Chesnuts will pay you, of course. We can do point-and-shoots at the rehearsal party tonight, but we need some professional portraits and candids tomorrow. . . . Oh, you will? Olivia, you are the best! I'll check with you later on logistics."

"I didn't know Olivia does photography," Bonnie said when I was off the phone.

"Well, she's got a nice digital," I said. "And she does have experience, although not with weddings."

"What with, then?" Bonnie handed me the last silver bell.

"Crime-scene photos. Don't tell Beth."

CHAPTER SIXTEEN

Stormy Weather

A gust of wind followed me up from the Coach House to Pinckney. Any minute, the heavens were going to open as the promised storm finally arrived.

Thank goodness, the last guests were gone, having driven away into the thick, still dark. The best man had still been talking about a few beers on the beach, but the rest of the bridal party was headed for bed, hoping to make it home before the bad weather. Beth was on automatic pilot. Another disaster and she'd be wearing a straitjacket tomorrow instead of the tasteful lilac MOB dress Mam had helped her pick out.

The wind picked up again, and the lights I'd just turned on flickered. Out the window, I saw a flashlight bobbing toward the back porch. There was a crash of thunder, then a loud pop. Darn, there went the power.

"Lindsey, where are you? Can you see?" Mam was banging on the kitchen door. "Let me in!" I found the doorknob. Mam stumbled in, dropping the flashlight as the wind slammed the door behind her. "It's starting to hail," she said, bumping into me and the kitchen table. "Can you find the flashlight? I got hit smack on my forehead. I think I'm bleeding."

"Stand still," I ordered. "You don't want to get any on your new dress." She scrunched up her eyes as I shone the light in her face. "There's no blood, but you've got a goose egg."

"That hail is as big as eggs, or at least golf balls. Listen! The azaleas are doomed." She grabbed the flashlight from me. "Let me go see how bad my face looks."

I followed her into the hall. "Give me the flashlight so I can get a couple candles going. The storm blew up too fast."

"Just a sec." Mam crouched to examine her forehead in the petticoat table mirror, where Southern belles had once checked the length of their crinolines. "Maybe it won't turn black and blue. I need a big knot on my face like a hole in my head." The flashlight, which had been growing dim, chose that moment to die. "Oh, good grief. What next?"

I could hear Mam starting to stand up. "Look out you don't crack your head on the table," I said. "And watch where you're swinging that flashlight. I think there are some batteries in the kitchen drawer."

"I'll follow you," Mam said, grabbing my shoulder and stepping on the back of my heel.

"Okay, careful." I thrust my arms in front of me, trying to visualize any objects in our path. It was blackest midnight in the hallway. My right hand found the doorjamb into the kitchen. "The door's right here." A flash of lightning illuminated the kitchen, allowing me to get my bearings.

"Don't you have another flashlight?" Mam asked.

"A little one on a key chain. It's in my purse."

"Where's your purse?"

"Right here on the table." I groped. Wallet. Lipstick. Sunglasses. Didn't need those. "Aha!" A tiny beam of light. I aimed it at the drawer where we kept candles, then directed Mam toward the fridge. "Grab that dishtowel and put some ice on your forehead so it doesn't swell."

"It seems funny to put ice on something ice caused in the first place." Mam moved to the window by the door. "J. T. and Posey were dragging the urns with the palms into the stable. I hope they have the sense to stay put."

"Where's Bonnie?"

"Still in the Coach House, helping Mike load the catering van," Mam said. "Thank goodness Cissy's at home with Ashley."

The lightning flashed again, and Mam gasped. What the . . . ? She opened the kitchen door, and someone barreled through it, trailing the faintly metallic scent of rain and ozone.

"Goodness, I didn't think I'd make it!" Bonnie was winded from running. "The lights were still on when I started. Good thing it's a straight shot up the back drive."

"Why on earth did you run up here?" Mam shoved the door shut as the spatter of drops increased. "You could have gotten creamed."

"I had protection." She laughed, holding a silver hors d'oeuvre tray over her head. "See, I'm not a dumb blonde."

"You're not really a blonde," Mam retorted. "You might have been hit by lightning, or broken an ankle in those sandals. It's getting worse out there."

"I know. That's why I came. Mike had the radio on in his van, and there's a tornado warning for the whole island. I thought I'd be safer in the basement here than in the Coach House with all those windows."

"What about Mike?" Mam took the tray from Bonnie and ran her hand over it to check for hail damage.

"He ran to the stables to warn the guys they should stay there. At least it's brick, like the basement here. Come on, I think we ought to go downstairs."

"Let me get the candles."

Thunder drowned my voice. Sideways rain pelted the windows. The wind banged a loose shutter. The storm was on top of us.

"No time!" Bonnie yelled. She yanked open the door to the back stairs. "Lindsey, you've got the light. Come here so we can see the steps."

I followed the two of them, aiming my pitiful excuse for a flash-

140

light at Bonnie's feet and hanging onto the banister with my other hand. Just as I reached the bottom, I felt a blast of cold air. The door at the top of the stairs slammed shut.

"Why did you close the door?" Mam asked nervously.

"I didn't. It must have been the wind," I said.

"Well, go open it before I get claustrophobia."

Bonnie shouldered her way past me back up the wooden stairs. "I'll get it. Wait, it's stuck. The wind must have jammed it. It's warped anyway. Or maybe it's the air pressure. It does funny things during tornadoes."

"I don't think it's a tornado," I said. "At least not yet."

"Oh, I forgot. You were in one that summer you went to the Girl Scout arts camp at that college in Kansas. Did it really sound like a train?"

"Sort of," I said. "But we were in a real basement underground, not just under a house. They had warning sirens like for an air raid. The counselors herded us down the stairs, and then we all sat in a circle and sang songs. It was typical Girl Scout stuff—singing *Boom-dee-ada, Boom-dee-ada* while the sky was falling."

"It's booming pretty bad here." Bonnie took the flashlight from me and beamed its thin light around the downstairs room, picking out the junk piled in the gloom.

Like other old sea-island plantation houses, Pinckney was built high off the ground. Years ago, though, the area beneath the kitchen and front parlor had been bricked. It became a repository for bulk supplies and, over time, an appliance tomb. An ancient vacuum leaned in one dusty corner, next to an old wringer washing machine and a rusted freezer. It was my least favorite part of Pinckney, except for the attic.

"Are you breathing okay, Mam?" I asked.

"Yes, it's really not that bad. There's plenty of cool air down here. And I know I could go through that outside door if I wanted to, which I don't. Mercy, it's raining to beat the band. And look at the lightning through the grates!"

It was as if someone was flicking a switch on and off.

"I'm beginning to think you're walking under a dark cloud, Mam,"

I teased. She wiped off the bottom stairsteps with her dishtowel so we'd have a place to sit. "Things keep happening when you're around."

Bonnie gingerly sat on the last step. "Mama says you're an accident waiting to happen."

"Hush your mouth!" Mam snapped the dishtowel at her. "Scoot up the stairs, so Lindsey and I can sit. We're all in this together. We all found Lorna and the pot. And it was Lindsey who found MaryMar's stalker and Lorna's killer."

"I found Scott's car," I corrected her.

"Same difference."

"Scott killed Lorna," Bonnie chimed in.

"This is a dry-clean-only dress." Mam swished the towel across the step again before sitting down. "Who else would have killed her? Scott was definitely stalking MaryMar."

"Yeah, but why kill Lorna?" The question had been troubling me all day. "As many pictures as he took of MaryMar, he knew the difference between the two. That whole idea of her being mistaken for MaryMar doesn't work. Besides, he was a Peeping Tom with that camera, but he didn't really threaten MaryMar."

"That's true," Bonnie put in. "All the notes said was 'Smile. I'm watching you.' That's kind of creepy, but it's not like he was out to murder her. Whoever heard of the Say-Cheese Killer?"

"He's crazy," Mam said firmly. "Who knows what he was thinking? He was obsessed with her. He probably knew she has a thing with Ron. Maybe Scott was jealous, although then I guess he would have killed Ron." She shook her head. "No, somehow Lorna figured out he was the stalker, and Scott knew she knew, so he had to get rid of her before she turned him in. Or she could have been trying to blackmail him."

"That's total speculation." Bonnie loved playing devil's advocate. "Let's look at the facts. Lorna overdosed on alcohol and Xanax, or so we hear. A full toxicology report takes time. And they still haven't released her body."

"They haven't even officially said she's dead," I noted. "You know, it could be an accident. Lorna slid off the wagon into MaryMar's meds and then had a couple of drinks."

"But they found that pill bottle in Scott's glove compartment." Mam was ready to send him to the slammer.

"A lot of people take Xanax. The evidence is circumstantial." Bonnie aimed the flashlight toward the grate. "Is it my imagination, or is the storm getting worse?"

A crash of thunder made us jump. Bonnie was right. The wind was whining now, the rain gushing through rattling drainpipes.

"Circumstantial evidence is key," Mam said. "You need to watch *CSI.*" She stood and started pacing. "I can't believe this storm is happening right before the wedding."

"Better than during." I wished she'd sit back down. She was making me antsy.

Bonnie, too. "Sit down, Mam. You're liable to trip over some of the stuff that's down here."

"It's a good thing we were waiting till tomorrow to put up the tent. The wind would have carried it off by now." Mam perched on the bottom step next to me. "As it is, Lonnie's going to have to spray all over again, or the gnats will eat us alive." She tapped her foot. "All this rain is going to make the ground soft, too. I can just see the bathroom trailer getting stuck in the mud." She twisted her hair. "I hope J. T.'s all right. He's probably freaking out worrying about me. He knows I hyperventilate when I'm in closed-up spaces."

"We all know you're claustrophobic," Bonnie said with a sigh. "I remember the time when we were little and Mama and Daddy took us to those caves in Tennessee. They turned out the lights, and all we could hear was you gasping."

"It was horrible." Mam shuddered. "It was like being buried alive."

"We can try opening the door to under the house," Bonnie said. "You'd have more fresh air, but we'd still have a roof over our heads."

"I don't think that's a good idea," I said quickly. "There are probably all sorts of critters taking shelter. We don't want to invite them in here." I wasn't sure what would be worse, Mam passing out from lack of oxygen or from coming face to face with a snake. "Listen, it's slacking off."

Another loud boom made a liar out of me. Then came a crashing noise from overhead.

"What was that?" Mam trembled next to me. "Is there somebody upstairs?"

"Maybe a limb hit the house." I looked at the ceiling. No matter how often Pinckney was sprayed for bugs, it was a haven for spiders. If one dropped on me, I'd freak out. "Or maybe a shutter came loose. This house has survived worse storms than this."

Bonnie patted Mam on the shoulder. "Remember, Posey takes good care of this place. He has to answer to Miss Augusta."

Mam laughed weakly. "She's scarier than any thunderstorm. I wouldn't want to be MaryMar when Miss Augusta starts lecturing her about having an affair with a married man."

"Maybe Ron will make an honest woman out of her," I said hopefully. "Maybe she'll stop trying to cozy up to other guys."

"I doubt it." Bonnie played with the flashlight, using it like a laser pointer. "She always wants to be the center of attention. Ron may be getting a trophy wife, but he could turn out to be just her starter husband." The flashlight beam bounced off the walls, picking out a bicycle pump and a kid's red wagon, jumping to the stacks of paper towels, climbing to the grate above. "Look!" Bonnie yelped, her knees pushing into my back as she stood up. "There's somebody out there! I can see his face!"

Chapter Seventeen

Partly Cloudy with Clearing Later

"Face it, Bonnie, no one's there." I shone the flashlight's thin beam at the grate again. In the excitement, she'd dropped the light, which conveniently landed in my lap. "See? No one, nothing, nada."

"Not now," Bonnie said stubbornly. "But I tell you, I saw the whites of his eyes. Somebody was out there!"

"Well, they're not there now," Mam said. "You scared them off when you screamed."

"I did not scream. That was you. I just raised my voice."

"I screamed because you yelled. Isn't that right, Lindsey?"

Why did I have to be the arbiter? "At least y'all made noise. I couldn't get any sound to come out of my mouth."

"So you did see something!" Bonnie was triumphant.

"I don't know. Honest. There was the flashlight, the lightning, y'all screaming. Then it was dark." It had all happened in an instant. "Whoever or whatever is long gone. And the storm's almost over." Lightning still lit up the night, but the thunder was a mere grumble now.

Just as I felt my shoulders easing, there was a pounding at the door to the outside. Mam jumped back to huddle with us on the stairs.

"Should we open it?" Bonnie asked.

"Who's there?" Mam said. "Identify yourself!"

"It's me." J. T.'s voice sent Mam running to the door.

"Oh, I'm so glad to see you!" Mam threw herself on her husband. "Are you all right? You're all wet."

"I'm fine, just a little damp. How about you girls?" He held up the lantern in his hand and looked at Bonnie and me. We both nodded. I exhaled in relief. "Where's Posey?" J. T. asked. "We left for up here as soon as we thought it was safe. I got tangled up in a branch, though. There's a lot of debris. Still, he should have been here by now."

Noise overhead startled us all. The stairway door burst open, and another lantern loomed out of the dark. "Y'all down there?"

Posey!

"We're here!" I called. "Come on down and join the party."

"Why don't y'all come up here? That way, I won't drip all over the stairs. And I know Lindsey's not much on that basement."

"No kidding." I hurriedly followed Bonnie up the stairs. "Those are great lanterns. I didn't know we had any."

"I bought them at Costco during hurricane season. Put a couple down at the stable, and brought two up here. Marietta must have them in the hall closet."

"Let me have the little flashlight, Lindsey, and I'll go get them." Bonnie grinned. "I need to go to the ladies' anyhow. Posey, you sure scared us, looking in the grate like that."

"What are you talking about?" Posey asked sharply. "I wasn't at no grate. I came right up the back porch. Did y'all see something? J. T., you roaming round underneath the house?"

"No, just beating on the door so they'd let me in."

"Where's Mike?" Bonnie asked. "Maybe it was him. But he was going down to the stables to tell you guys to stay there 'cause there was a tornado warning."

"He wasn't with us." J. T. frowned, the lantern light turning his face into a Halloween mask. "We better go look for him. He's probably in one of the other outbuildings, or maybe he stayed in the Coach House."

Posey headed for the door. "Probably so. I want to see if we got any trees down. Good thing that wedding reception's not till tomorrow night. We got a lot of cleaning up to do."

J. T. waited until we turned on a lantern from the hall closet, then dropped a quick kiss on Mam's head. "What's that on your forehead? Are you hurt?"

"Just a little hail bump," she said. "It's nothing. At least it's not a hole in my head."

J. T. snorted. "Or in your hair."

"What's he talking about?" I said, shutting the door behind him. The storm had sure cooled things off.

"Oh, it's no big deal. I don't know why he said that."

"Said what?" Bonnie asked, returning to the kitchen.

"Something about a hole in Mam's hair." I took a lantern from Bonnie. Maybe there was a Coke in the fridge.

"Oh, didn't she tell you about her little Mam moment this morning?" Bonnie giggled. "It was right after you left. She yelled at me to come help her because she'd cut her hair with J. T.'s hedge trimmers."

"J. T.'s hair trimmers." Mam looked abashed. "I said hedge trimmers by mistake. I was trying to cut that little rat tail at the back of my wedge, and I ended up cutting this huge hunk of hair. Bonnie fixed it so you can hardly notice." She turned her back so I could see.

The phone rang, and we all stared at it in amazement.

Mam picked up the black receiver. "Pinckney Plantation . . . Hey, Cissy . . . No, we don't have any power either, but everybody's fine. We'll get home just as soon as we can. And if the lights aren't on by then, Daddy'll get the generator going. . . . Okay, I'll call her. . . . Yes, I expect she is. Bye, sweetie."

She turned to us. "Looks like there's no power on the island, but the phones are working, if you've got a land line. Beth called, and Cissy says she sounded pretty upset." She sighed. "I think I'll wait to call her till we know more. Is that J. T. back already? And who's that with him?"

Bonnie opened the door. J. T. trooped in, followed by a man in a dripping poncho. Lonnie Williams shoved the hood off his head, breathing heavily.

"We didn't know you were still here." Mam handed Lonnie a dishtowel so he could mop his face and matted hair. "Did y'all find Mike?"

"He and Posey are getting the chain saws from the shed," J. T. said. "And we need to see if we can get the Bobcat running."

"There's a big pine down at the end of the drive," Lonnie explained with a wheeze. "It's completely blocking the road. I almost ran into it as I went around the curve going out. Five minutes earlier, I might have been under it." His arm trembled as he held out the dishtowel to Mam. "Sorry, I think I better, uh . . ."

"Sit down." I shoved a chair under him. If Lonnie passed out in the kitchen, it would be like an oak falling.

"Drink this," Mam said, handing him a glass of water.

Lonnie gulped it gratefully. He shuddered, drops of water flying from the dark green poncho. "I'll be okay. I just sat in the van, hoping there wasn't another tree." He exhaled. "I don't like being shut in like that. I always drive with a window open, even when it's cold."

"I know what you mean," Mam said sympathetically. "I get claustrophobic, too. When I was little, I was in a cave—"

Bonnie interrupted her. "Are y'all going to try to move that tree tonight, J. T.? That doesn't sound safe."

"Probably not." J. T. seemed unperturbed. "But we don't have much choice if we want to get home. We'll use the headlights from the truck and see if we can't at least move enough off the drive to get through, then use the Bobcat tomorrow. Mam, I need you to call dispatch and see if they've had reports of other trees blocking roads."

"Is there anything Bonnie and I can do?" I asked.

J. T. surveyed us in our party dresses and sandals. His khakis were streaked with rain, his shoes muddy. "Y'all can come aim headlights and hold lanterns, I guess." He cocked his head. "But not you, Mam. After seeing what you did with my clippers, I'm not letting you anywhere near a chain saw."

The morning was damp and chilly, the buzz of chain saws competing with the songbirds as I drove toward the beach. The clean smell of pine sap scented the air.

Daylight revealed palm fronds, broken branches, twigs, and leaves scattered everywhere. The azaleas at Middle House had taken a battering. The pink blooms not on the ground looked like valiant little rags. Standing water pooled on the shoulder of the road, spilling onto the blacktop in low places.

The power was still out, which was why I was headed to the Beachside Café. Owners Tiny and Eula had some sort of super generator and always did a brisk business after a storm. Although I rarely ate a hot breakfast, I had awakened with a hankering for a country ham biscuit. The café's biscuits weren't as light as Marietta's, but jelly dabbed on the salty meat still made a mouth-watering combo. I'd fed the animals and dressed quickly, hoping to get out of the house before Mam called.

The parking lot indicated a full house, but as I pushed open the glass door, I spotted an empty vinyl stool at the end of the counter. Sometimes, Will and I met here, slipping into a booth at the back. I'd talked to him briefly last night after finally getting home.

"The north end of the island got the worst of it, as far as I can tell," he'd reported. "There was a waterspout in the sound, and Turner Hickey claims a tornado touched down near Cottonmouth. I'm on my way there now. The rest of the county's fine. It hardly even rained in Centerville. The power company hopes to have everybody up by midday."

"Promises, promises. I'll believe it when I see the lights come on," I said. "You sound tired. Are you going to get any sleep?"

"I hope I can grab a few hours in the morning. Earl Crosby's taking my Saturday-night shift."

"So you'll be at the wedding?" It was out before I could stop myself. I was trying to be as devil-may-care as possible as to his whereabouts, already preparing myself for the long absence.

"I'm going to try," he said. "I hear you corralled Olivia into taking pictures, so I may have to direct traffic."

I couldn't resist. "MaryMar's liable to bring traffic to a standstill in that bridesmaid's dress. You won't want to miss her in all her glory."

"I don't want to miss you. I'll be there."

"Promises, promises," I'd said airily, even though it was quite a satisfactory reply on his part. "I'll see you when I see you."

Now, I took a long drink of Coke from the red plastic tumbler Eula set in front of me without my asking. Around me, I heard bits of conversation about the storm and its aftermath.

"Lost the top off a palmetto."

"The tide was across the road."

"No, they said it wasn't a tornado but a microburst or some such."

"We didn't have any gas for the generator, and you know how long it takes to boil water on a grill."

If the power didn't come on soon, I'd have to set up the generator at Middle House or risk letting everything in the refrigerator and freezer spoil. Not that there was much to lose. Mama and Daddy's was another story. I'd have to tote everything over to the big freezer at Pinckney, which would be near empty come evening. It was just as well the wedding was tonight, or we'd be eating Marietta's *petits fours* and ham biscuits for days—not a bad idea, come to think of it.

Just then, my biscuit arrived, along with two tiny tubs of strawberry jam. "I know you like it better than grape jelly," Eula said.

She refilled my neighbor's coffee cup. A young guy with short brown hair, a round, open face, and a solid set of shoulders, he was methodically eating his way through the breakfast special. He'd nodded when I sat down. He looked familiar, though I couldn't place him. Then it came to me that he was a groomsman from the rehearsal party last night, the one from Clemson who was to be Cissy's blind date. Hmm. He ought to take her mind off Jimmy.

Eula grabbed the phone behind the counter on its third ring.

"Beachside . . . Yes, here." She thrust the phone in my direction. "Be quick. I can't serve with that cord stretched across my prep area." Her nylons swished as she made for the cash register.

"Meet Bonnie at the beach." Mam's voice was so loud I held the phone a couple inches from my ear. "We have to move—no, Cissy, that purple tablecloth—the fish right away."

"The goldfish? I thought they weren't going into the brandy snifters till it was time to go down the aisle." Raising my voice over the clatter of Tiny clearing a table behind me, I caught several nearby diners' attention.

"Not goldfish!" Mam barked. "Jellyfish. There's a bunch of them washed up on the beach where the wedding's going to be. Bonnie will meet you with J. T.'s truck."

"Won't the tide carry them off this afternoon?"

"It's not going to come up high like during the storm."

"And you're doing"—I paused for emphasis—"*what?*" Why couldn't *she* pick jellyfish off the beach? I wanted to finish my biscuit in peace. How had she found me, anyway? Was I wearing a tracking device?

"I'm at Pinckney setting up the tables before the cake lady arrives. She's running behind. She's got hives, but she says she's had them before. As long as the cake doesn't get them, I don't care. She can just take a Benedryl and get her butt over here. No, Cissy, the dark purple."

I handed Eula the phone as she sailed by with the coffeepot. "Thanks. Can I get a to-go cup for the rest of this Coke? I need to go deal with some fish."

"The fishing's not going to be any good today," an elderly man waiting to take my seat at the counter pronounced loudly.

"Yes, sir," I said. "But these fish have already landed. I'm on cleanup duty."

"You need a sharp knife to clean fish." He took off his cap as he sat down, and I saw the hearing aid almost hidden by a tuft of yellow-white hair. "It's kind of messy for a girl."

I sighed as I picked up my Coke. "These are jellyfish."

"Jelly!" His voice followed me out the door. "I like grape."

CHAPTER EIGHTEEN

Marching Orders

"Hideous," I said.

"Disgusting," said Bonnie.

We looked at each other, then at the flamingo-pink beach house with grape shutters and trim.

"Too tacky for words," I said.

"More money than taste," agreed Bonnie. "Do you think it'll fade over the summer?"

"Not nearly enough." I pulled on the gardening gloves Bonnie had brought me. "I hear the neighbors up here at the Point are trying to petition for a repaint, at least the purple part."

"Good luck to 'em." Bonnie was holding a black plastic trash bag and a small shovel. "And speaking of disgusting . . ."

Dead jellyfish spotted the sand like deflated gray balloons.

"At least they don't smell yet." I took the shovel and scooped one glutinous cannonball into the garbage bag. "We can take turns with the shovel, working from the tide mark to the water's edge. It really did come up high."

"Sue Beth might want to reconsider going barefoot." Bonnie shielded her eyes from the sun with her hand, surveying the beach. "A lot of junk washed up besides jellyfish."

"Flotsam and jetsam." Another jellyfish went into the bag, along with some trailing seaweed and dead man's fingers. "We'll do what we can in the next hour or so, but then I've got to get to Pinckney. I'm sure Miss Augusta's already talked to Posey and Marietta, but she'll still expect me to report in, too."

We worked steadily, but the jellyfish appeared to replicate even as we shoveled them into the bags. Poor creatures. Death dulled their rainbow iridescence to a pink dishwater hue. Riders on the storm. The sun burned through the early-morning haze, and I stopped to shrug off my sweatshirt and tie it round my waist.

"Phish," Bonnie said suddenly. "Remind me to ask Mam."

"Jellyfish or goldfish?"

"Neither. I want to know if she's answered any e-mails lately from banks or financial companies asking her to verify her personal information. That's how identity thieves often work, through phony e-mails. It's called phishing, with a *ph*."

"I've heard about it. I even got something from a credit-card company, but it wasn't my credit card, so I deleted it. You think maybe Mam took the bait?"

"Could be," Bonnie said. "Some of those e-mails look like the real thing. You have to be so careful these days. The information superhighway is not safe." She stopped to stretch and stood looking at the ocean. I wondered if she was missing Tom.

"Bonnie?"

"Mmm?"

"You use e-mail to stay in touch with Tom, don't you? I guess that makes it easier being separated."

"It's better now than when we were first married. When he was out on a cruise then, it could take a month to send a letter and get one back. And phone calls were really expensive, so we hardly ever talked.

Cell phones and computers make a big difference. There's a lot more communication in military marriages these days." She sighed. "Of course, it's not the same as him being home. The Navy has a good support system, but working and being a single parent is still hard. That's why I think I might come down here this summer, although rentals are so expensive. And I don't want to move in with Mom and Dad or Mam and J. T. There's not enough room. We're not good at sharing kitchens."

"You ought to live with me, since I hardly use mine. I know how to cook, but I don't." I poked at a small jellyfish almost indistinguishable from the speckled sand. "Actually, we might look for a place to rent together this summer, if Miss Maudie comes back to Middle House. Or if she decides to stay in Centerville, you and the boys could move in with me. I've got plenty of room."

Bonnie looked at me with surprise. "What about privacy? You already said it's hard for you and Will to have any time alone."

I grimaced. "*You* said that, but it's true. But that's not going to be a problem for a while. It seems Major McLeod is going off on some secret assignment the next few months. He just sprung it on me the other night."

"Hence your interest in long-distance communication." Bonnie looked at me seriously. "I'm sorry. You're probably worrying how his going off is going to affect your relationship."

"Something like that." It was my turn to stare at the ocean. "The timing is so lousy. We're still at the beginning of this thing. I mean, we may have known each other forever, but not since we were kids. There's a lot we don't know about each other. Like when MaryMar showed up. I was jealous of her, and I had no reason to be."

"MaryMar could make any woman feel insecure. I wouldn't want her around Tom, and it's not that I don't trust him. I just don't trust her not to try to cause trouble. You notice she doesn't have any girlfriends."

"She had Lorna."

"Some friend. I mean MaryMar, not Lorna. She used Lorna. She hasn't even asked about a funeral or anything. It's been all about Scott and Ron and the wedding."

"Well, they can't have a funeral anytime soon. Lorna's not dead, as far as most people know." I kicked a beer can. "Lord, what a mess. At least we're almost finished."

Bonnie picked up the can with disgust. "Look at this. Idiots everywhere."

"Uh-huh," I said, tying up the last bag. "Now what?"

"We haul the bags back up to J. T.'s truck, and I can either drop them at the dump or continue the cycle of life and empty the bags in the marsh for the coons." She rubbed her back and stretched. "Then I'll put the bags in recycling. After all, I have to practice what I preach."

"Whatever's fine with me. Look, Bonnie." I pointed to the ocean. "Dolphins."

"Where? Aw, I missed them." The black fins reappeared farther out. "There they are! A mama and her baby. Oh, cute. I wish the boys could see them. SeaWorld's great, but this is the real sea world."

I nodded, grateful for the breeze. "Looks like it'll be good weather for the wedding. With this many people already on the water, the landing's going to be backed up."

"Hey, is that the same yellow boat we saw at Lost Beach?"

I followed her gaze to where several boats were skimming past the channel markers. "It's hard to tell. As Will said, if a boat's not white, it's yellow."

"The yellow one's just sitting there idling. Doesn't Mike have a boat like that? I can see him secretly growing pot."

"You're prejudiced because of the ponytail." I picked up the shovel and the bag I'd just tied off. "Let's go. All boats look alike at this distance."

I trudged up the dune, watching my tennis shoes sink into the soft sand. The truck and my CR-V were parked at the Point's small public access area, another dune over. Bonnie followed, struggling to lift her heavier bag. She finally gave up and dragged it behind her.

"Whatcha got there, a dead body?"

I jumped. Mike was heading down the boardwalk toward us. Obviously, he wasn't in the yellow boat. Still, he owned one. He had a truck, too. He also wore expensive outerwear for someone who worked part-time for a caterer and did odd jobs at the landing.

"Here, let me help you with that." Mike took both my bag and Bonnie's and tossed them effortlessly in the back of J. T.'s pickup. "Margaret Ann sent me out here to give you a hand, but it looks like I'm too late."

"Since when do you work for my sister?" Bonnie pulled off her gloves and stuck them in her back pocket.

"Oh, I don't, officially." Mike grinned. "I finished with the bar setup for the reception, and I can't pick up the food till later, so she volunteered me to come help with jellyfish. Now, how could I resist a chance to spend time with two lovely ladies?"

I groaned. "Mike, you are such a flirt. I bet you couldn't wait to get out of there before Mam roped you into tent duty or something worse."

"Guilty as charged." Mike held up his hands. "But don't hold it against me. Seriously, is there anything else here at the Point?"

"Nope." Bonnie tossed her blonde locks. "The beach—at least—is squeaky clean."

"Oh, don't mind Bonnie," I said. "She found a beer can. Litter makes her grumpy. Her environmental job, you know. Thanks for coming by. We'll see you later."

Bonnie waited until Mike had driven off. " 'Litter makes her grumpy'? What kind of fool did you make me out to be?"

"Sorry, it was all I could think of. You were kind of short with him."

"I don't trust him. He's too good looking."

"This from Bonnie the Beautiful?"

She laughed. "Oh, all right. I'm just seeing crooks everywhere these days. I'll meet you back at Pinckney."

"Go get some coffee first," I advised. "Then maybe you won't be so grumpy."

She stuck out her tongue before wheeling out of the parking lot.

J. T. was the one who looked grumpy as Bonnie carefully parked the Ford F-150 next to my CR-V near the Pinckney stables. He hated to let that truck out of his sight. Mam must have done some fast talking to borrow it for hauling jellyfish. She was on the back porch now, waving her arms at us and yelling something. Fortunately, no tourists were around to see her acting like a crazy woman. After consulting with Posey last night, I'd made an executive decision not to open Pinckney to tourists before the power came back on. It was too dangerous because of all the storm debris. I'd thought Miss Augusta might protest, but she agreed immediately. "I don't want any more accidents at Pinckney," she'd fretted. "My insurance rates are sky-high as it is."

Bonnie climbed out of the truck. "Oh, my. Have you seen the rose garden yet?"

"No, but I've got my fingers crossed." I held them up to show her. "The live oaks don't look too bad. They're still standing, anyway. Posey says most of the damage is superficial."

J. T. rubbed his chin and looked at the back lawn, carpeted with curling strands of moss, broken branches, and new green twigs mixed in with the brown oak leaves that always fell this time of year. "Well, I better get to it." His voice was resigned. Posey had gotten to the Bobcat first, moving the broken pine trees so the drive was clear. Now, we needed chain saws, rakes, and wheelbarrows—and people willing to work up a sweat.

"Didn't you hear me?" Mam came to stand beside us. "Wiley called. He and the groomsmen are coming over to help for a couple hours. First, they have to take some extra generators over to Beth's and the house where the bridesmaids are. They need them for all the blow-dryers. Lucille's already starting on hair." She looked at Bonnie and me. "Y'all can help me with flowers. J. T., can you check on the chandeliers?"

"I already did," he said. "One of the limbs is down, but the chandelier's intact. The others are still in place, but we'll make sure they're secure. You'll need some more candles, though. And two globes are broken."

"Great," Mam said.

Did she mean *great* as in "Great, now I have to find two more globes" or "What a great husband you are, J. T."? Probably some of both. She loved her black iron chandeliers. And they did look magical at night, the lights swaying among the oaks.

"Tiki torches," Mam said now. "J. T., ask Posey where they are. We might have to use them." She started back up toward the house, our very own Energizer bunny. "Marietta, can you hear me? I need ten short white tapers, new if possible."

Bonnie and I looked at one another and headed toward the basement door. We had our marching orders. My back ached. I tried not to be in Mam's vicinity on days she did weddings. Her bark was worse than her bite, but it was all the barking that got to me. Heaven help us when Cissy got married. Maybe I'd encourage an elopement. Mam always was willing to go the extra mile, even for her princess brides, which was why she was in such demand. But I already had walked those extra miles—and back again—picking up jellyfish on the beach. As Uncle James said, my feet were tired of passing each other.

Marietta was in the basement as we came in the outside door. Even in daylight, with the door wide open, it was gloomy.

"I think the candles are in the kitchen," I said. Margaret Ann was up there now, barking at somebody on the phone.

Marietta nodded. "I know candles are upstairs. I came down so's to get away from the noise. Somethin' 'bout a cake."

"I've been there already." And I wasn't interested in going again. "Marietta, how did your garden survive the storm?"

"It's right pitiful looking now, beaten down by the rain, but I reckon it'll all grow back. The cherry tomatoes are the worst."

"What about the Pinckney Plant?" Bonnie asked.

"You know about Pinckney Plant? Most young folks don't. My granny's the one told me 'bout it. Said it was good for pain. I found some over near the graveyard and planted the seeds last year. It grows fast."

"Does it work?" I asked.

"I only try it a long time ago. My granny smoked it in a pipe. And one time, I had female trouble something terrible. The pain went away, but I didn't much like feelin' all slow and dopey." *Dopey* was the word. Marietta would be surprised how many young people knew all about Pinckney Plant. "Why you down here?" she asked.

"We're supposed to help with the flowers." Bonnie looked around. "I need that old red wagon to haul centerpieces. I thought I saw it down here last night."

"Posey already took care of it. You know, he never go home last night. He called Vanessa, and she told him to stay, she and the girls were fine. I got me a ride over here at first light, and he hard at it."

"I hope he takes a break." Pinckney needed him. I could handle the house and the tours, but no one else knew the plantation acreage like Posey.

"Mam will want us at the Coach House, then." Bonnie looked at me. "We'll have to wrap the columns with ivy."

The door upstairs swung open, silhouetting Margaret Ann at the top of the stairs. "Marietta, did you find the candles? Bonnie, go up to the Coach House and help Cissy with the ivy. Lindsey, come call Olivia and tell her to be at the Chesnuts' by four, so she can take pictures of Sue Beth getting dressed." She clapped her hands. "Let's move it. We've got a wedding to put on!"

There she was with that *we* again. Bonnie looked at me and shrugged.

"Yes, Mam!" we shouted up the stairs. "*We* know!"

CHAPTER NINETEEN

Wedding Belles

"We are gathered here today to join this man and this woman . . ."

As the minister spoke the familiar words, I looked out at the crowd. The family and older folks were seated in rows of white chairs that were only slightly off kilter because of the way the beach sloped. The rest of us stood behind them and at the side of the dune as the sunset provided a glorious backdrop to the Chesnut-Day nuptials.

So far, there'd been no obvious mishaps. Sue Beth, in her froth of meringue, her face radiant, seemed to be walking on air instead of flip-flops. No way was she going to let MaryMar upstage her. Lucille had helped in that regard, lacquering MaryMar's platinum tresses to her head so that from a distance she resembled a Q-tip in a purple dress. The thirteenth bridesmaid was on her best behavior, probably because she knew Ron was among the onlookers. Elise, we'd heard, was on her way to Puerto Rico in the company of her divorce attorney.

I punched Bonnie with the fan that doubled as a program and

mouthed, "I'm going." I needed to get back to Pinckney ahead of the reception crowd and had accordingly parked the CR-V for a quick getaway.

Driving off the Point and finding the road lined on either side with cars and trucks, I came face to face with a dark green pickup. Turner was late for the wedding. I waited for him to reverse so I could get out. "Thanks. I have to get to Pinckney." It was the first time I'd seen him since he'd driven Scott up to the marsh. He looked old and tired.

"I reckon I might as well turn around and follow you," he said, leaning out the window. "By the time I find a place to park here, it'll probably be over."

I smiled and waved good-bye.

There wasn't much traffic on King's Road, since everyone was at the wedding, but I still turned off at Crab Creek to take the back way into Pinckney. I was surprised when Turner's truck turned as well. Of course, an old-timer would know all the shortcuts.

Allgood's catering vans were parked near the Coach House. I pulled in next to Posey's truck by the stables. Signs pointed to the portable toilet trailers discreetly hidden by a stand of pines that, thankfully, were still standing. The white tent stood out against the darkening sky, Mam's chandeliers twinkling like fireflies. The band was doing a sound check. Its van was almost identical to that of Hired Killers, minus the cockroach. It was fortunate that the electricity had come on around noon, since the island probably didn't have enough generators to power the guitars and amplifiers.

"You can't even tell there was a storm," Turner marveled at my elbow. "We've got a ways to go at the Gatortorium yet."

"I heard you were hit pretty hard." I was heading quickly toward the Coach House, per Mam's instructions. Until she arrived, I was the catering and reception liaison. Bonnie had volunteered, but Mam had put her in charge of the bridal party after the ceremony. She would shepherd them through a photo session with Olivia while Mam oversaw the troops. J. T. would be stationed in the parking area. Marietta would stand guard at the house, which was closed to visitors. Posey would . . . I couldn't remember what Posey's assignment was.

"A couple windows were smashed at Lizard Lodge, and the rain came in." Turner kept step beside me. He was wearing his alligator boots. "Then a big tree limb landed in the pit, tore the mesh some. I think we may have lost some blacksnakes."

"Don't tell Mam," I said.

Turner chuckled. "That reminds me. Y'all got a big blacksnake living under that shed by the graveyard. I'll be happy to take it off your hands." I stumbled, and Turner quickly caught me before I nosedived. "You all right? Didn't turn your ankle?"

"No, no, I'm fine," I said brightly. "That's what I get for wearing heels. Thanks." What did Turner know about the graveyard shed? There weren't any gators—ghost or otherwise—in that part of Pinckney. "You'll have to ask Posey about the snake. If it were up to me, you could have all of 'em. But he's the groundskeeper."

Turner nodded. "Snakes keep down your rodent population. Natural pest control."

Talk about pests. I needed to get rid of him. Mam would be here soon, and I didn't want to be derelict in my duty. "Oh, there's the cake lady," I said, spying a large woman with a white chef's apron tied over a vivid floral dress. She looked straight out of a Jonathan Green painting. "Turner, I'll see you later. Have a good time."

"The cake's good," Bonnie said, licking her fork. "The icing's that fondant stuff, though—pretty but not much taste." She considered her empty glass plate. "I think I liked the crab puffs best. The fish fingers sure went fast."

"Don't mention fish to me." Mam plopped into a folding chair next to Bonnie and me. "And swear to me that you'll never let a bride talk me into goldfish bouquets at a beach wedding. Oh, Lordy, what a scene!"

We'd forgotten about the seagulls. Several had arrived just before I departed the beach. When she started telling me what happened next, Bonnie laughed so hard she cried.

"Here, wipe your face," I said, handing her one of the napkins with "Sue Beth & Wiley" printed on it. "Your waterproof mascara isn't. You've got raccoon eyes."

Bonnie dabbed her eyes, still chortling. "Whoo-ee! I tell you, I had to cross my legs. You should have seen it."

"Seen what?" All I'd gotten out of her so far was something about a gull, a goldfish, and MaryMar.

"So Sue Beth and Wiley were marching back down the aisle, and everyone's smiling and clapping. Then the bridesmaid behind MaryMar, who should have been at the end, but Mam lined them up by height, so MaryMar was in the middle . . ." Bonnie started laughing again. "It was so funny!"

"What? What?"

Bonnie took a deep breath. "The bridesmaid tripped—I don't know on what, maybe we missed a jellyfish—but then when she threw up her arms to catch her balance, her poor goldfish went sailing through the air. It went right over MaryMar's shoulder and landed smack dab in her cleavage! You should have seen it, Lindsey. That fish was head down, and the only thing you could see was this itty-bitty tail wiggling in the last ray of sun. Wait! There's more." She put the napkin to her mouth as she started to giggle. "Here came this seagull. It must have seen the fish fly through the air 'cause it started diving for MaryMar. She stopped dead and started squealing and squealing until Cissy, sitting there on the end, reached over and plucked out the little fish and tossed it up to the gull so he'd go away. He missed it but did manage to poop on MaryMar's head. Poor thing!"

"Poor thing, my foot," I said. "She made our lives miserable the past few days. What goes around comes around."

"I meant the gull." Bonnie flapped an elbow. "It got so scared by everybody yelling and waving their arms that it flew away without any dinner."

"What about the goldfish?"

"It landed in MaryMar's brandy snifter, so she had two of 'em. Ron took it from her, because by that time she realized there was doo-doo in her hair, and she was about to have hysterics. Oh, it was priceless!"

"At least it happened at the end of the wedding," I said to Mam, who'd sat dejectedly through Bonnie's account. "It could have been worse."

"Don't I know it." Mam shook her head, then smiled. "It *was* funny, and Beth and Sunny were laughing as hard as anybody. Sue Beth didn't seem to mind either that MaryMar was stealing her thunder for a minute, 'cause MaryMar looked the perfect fool." She sighed. "And all's well that ends well, 'cause Ron whisked MaryMar out of there, and they still haven't come to Pinckney. She didn't stick around for the photo session either."

"But that's okay," Bonnie said. "Olivia got it on video. You'll have to see it, Lindsey."

"Maybe MaryMar can use it as an audition tape." I was happy she hadn't made the reception. Then again, neither had Will. I guessed he was still working. Now, the social event of the year was on its last legs. Most of the guests had departed after Sue Beth and Wiley drove off to Charleston in his SUV. Their plane for Cancun left tomorrow. Brook had caught the bouquet as planned, and she and her fiancé were among the last on the dance floor, even as Allgood's cleanup crew rounded up glasses and plates.

"Lindsey, I'm going to get the bill from Lonnie so I can put it in the file for Beth," Mam said. "He's not going to charge her for the respray today, but I'm going to see she gives him some money for helping us with the tent and everything. I think he's down with J. T. now, helping get the cars out."

"What have we got left?" Bonnie asked.

"Not much," Mam said. "We can return the palms in the morning before the church service. Didn't Posey say he'd do the tent in the morning, too?"

"Uh-huh," I said, yawning. "We have to have everything back in order by noon so we can open the plantation." I rested my eyes. I was tired of all this wedding stuff. Just running Pinckney would be a cinch after this.

"Did you save the last dance for me?"

I opened my eyes. Will was standing in front of me, holding out his hand. Bonnie had dragged Mam away toward the kitchen.

The band was reprising "My Girl" as Will and I drifted into a slow shag. I let him dip me at the end, knowing he'd catch me.

"Hey," I said against his chest afterward as the strains of "Mood Indigo"—the traditional last dance on the island—floated on the evening air. "I'm glad you made it."

"Me, too." He pulled me closer.

"Did you hear about MaryMar? And what about Scott and Lorna?"

"Let's not talk about them." He danced me off the floor, pulling me out of the tent and into the shadows. The night air was fragrant with spring. There was jasmine nearby. "Turn around," Will said after a long kiss, "and pull you hair up off your neck. I've got something for you."

His fingers were warm as he fastened the clasp of a chain. By the light of Mam's chandelier, I saw the gleam of delicate silver. I felt for the small charm on my breastbone. "Is it a bell?"

Will turned me around. "A Southern belle in a hoop skirt. You may not like it, after yesterday, but I thought of you at Pinckney when I saw it at the jewelry store last week. Just in case, I bought another charm, too." He held out his hand under the light. A tiny silver alligator was nestled in his palm.

I smiled up at him. "I like them both. They're perfect."

CHAPTER TWENTY

Special Delivery

"They're perfect," I said.

"No, they're not." Mam glared at the floral arrangement in front of her, replacing a purple hydrangea with an Easter lily. "There. That will have to do. I'm running out of time."

"It's just seven o'clock," I said, leaning against the cooler in Mam's garage, watching her at the waist-high workbench. "It's barely sunrise. And why are you messing with flowers? The wedding's over."

"These are for the Episcopalians." She whipped her floral knife back and forth, shaping greenery. "See, if I put lilies with the leftover wedding flowers, I get a brand-new look."

"Uh-huh." I yawned.

It had still been dark when my phone rang, interrupting a really good dream about a man in uniform. "Do you have the keys to the Finches' bread truck?" Mam's voice had been so loud that Peaches' ears twitched. He must have been enjoying a good dream, too.

"I don't have them on me, but I know where they keep them," I'd mumbled, patting Doc's head. Now that he was awake, I'd have to get up and let him out. "Why?"

"Because something's wrong with my van, and we've got to get those palms for the Baptists. The urns won't fit in your CR-V."

"What about J. T.'s truck?"

"He took Cissy to the sunrise service. He won't be back in time, and I can't reach him on his cell. I think he turned it off."

I wished I could turn her off, but it was too late.

And so here I was now, in my work uniform of Pinckney sweatshirt, jeans, and Nikes. "Please tell me we don't have to deliver these arrangements, too."

"Nope. I'll leave J. T. a note," Mam said. "I was going to ask him earlier, but we don't talk in the mornings."

"You mean J. T. doesn't talk in the mornings. You talk in your sleep. Where's Bonnie?"

"Finishing her coffee." Mam gave the arrangement a final pat, then yelled up the stairs to the kitchen. "Bonnie, come on! Lindsey's here. Grab my purse off the counter, please." She turned back to me. "Of all days for the van not to start. We've got to get those palms and still have time to dress for church."

"I probably won't make it," I said. "Not if I have to open Pinckney by noon. That's okay. There'll be so many twice-a-years at the Methodists', they won't miss me."

Bonnie sauntered out the downstairs door in jeans and a purple Pinckney sweatshirt like mine. She had an oversized blue coffee cup with a flounder on the side. She took a sip and silently rolled her eyes at me. We watched as Mam bustled to put the arrangement in the cooler and hastily scrawled a note to J. T.

"Okay, I'm ready," she said. She took her new red Vera Bradley purse—an Easter gift from Bonnie—and marched out of the garage. "Where's the bread truck?"

"At the Finches', I told you."

"I thought you were going to pick it up on your way here."

"It's closer to Pinckney. Besides, you get to drive the thing. It's your idea." I backed the CR-V. All I could see in the rearview mirror was Mam's head. "Sit down, Mam. It seems like there'd be another truck we could borrow."

"I tried to call Posey, but he didn't answer." Mam fumbled with the seatbelt. "And I thought about calling the café, but Eula said she wasn't going to open till lunch. Then I remembered the bread truck. You do have the keys, right?"

"I know where they are."

⌒

"Lindsey, I thought you knew where the keys are." Mam's voice sounded shrill. "They're not here."

"Yes, they are." I reached above her head and tilted the hanging basket of plastic begonias. The keys fell out, clunking on the porch.

Mam picked them up. "When you said they were in the flower basket, I thought you meant real flowers. Those are fake." She shuddered.

"They're all fake."

"I hate fake flowers, at least those kind, although they do last longer at the cemetery. Some of the silk ones are nice enough, but they still don't have any smell." She stopped short as she reached the bread truck. "Phew! What's that smell, skunk?"

"More like bobcat." Bonnie wrinkled her nose. "That's what you get living out here in the middle of the woods. Where am I supposed to sit if Mam's driving?"

"You can either have the jump seat or the breadbox in the middle."

"Breadbox," Bonnie said, climbing in. "That jump seat is sprung."

"I feel like we ought to be stopping at the Pig and delivering bread." Mam popped the clutch. "What's that noise in the back? Something's sliding around. Lindsey, you said it was cleaned out."

"I thought it was." I turned and looked over my shoulder. "There's an old mattress backed up behind us. I can't see past it. But there should be plenty of rooms for the palms."

"I'll have to use the side mirrors," Mam groused, "and figure out these gears."

The bread truck jerked forward. Bonnie hung onto me as Mam stepped on the gas, launching us out of the driveway like some kind of rocket.

Bonnie chuckled. "Let's move these buns!"

"Switch places with me, Lindsey?"

"Why, do your buns hurt?"

"Ha ha. But yeah, my butt is going to sleep on this box." Bonnie moved restlessly.

"Hang on, we don't have far to go. We're on the back road now. We're not too far from the goddesses."

"It's no wonder no one uses this road." Bonnie craned her neck to look out. "I can't see the ruts, but I sure feel them."

"I'm doing the best I can." Mam looked at the side mirror. "This thing drives like a tank."

"Maybe you can trade in your van for a Humvee," I suggested.

"And paint it rose colored," Bonnie offered.

"The van's more practical for flowers." Mam thought we were serious. "Hey, Lindsey, look at your mirror. There's a truck flashing its lights behind us. Should I stop or pull over so it can get around?"

I saw the lights, too. And I heard a horn. "Do both. Let's see who it is."

Mam slowed, carefully edging the bread truck over to the ragged shoulder. But whoever it was didn't want to come around. A truck— no, it was a van—slowed to a stop behind us.

"I think it's Lonnie." I saw his sandy red hair as he opened the van door. "But he doesn't have the cockroach on top."

"Maybe it takes Easter off." Bonnie lifted herself from the box and then sat down again. "Y'all go see what he wants. My leg's cramping."

Lonnie was kneeling by our right rear tires. He looked up. "You ladies are getting a flat. Hop in my van and I'll take you where you need to go. We can get someone from the filling station to come fix it."

"No need for that. There's probably a jack in the back." Mam yanked on the handle and pulled the door open. "Do you see one?"

I didn't. What I saw was a jumble of hoses and tubing, a can of Red Devil lye, several jugs of kerosene, assorted buckets and cans, and packets of Sudafed. The stench of bobcat urine was overpowering. Only it wasn't bobcat. The bread truck was a portable meth lab. Oh, geez.

"I really wish you hadn't opened that door." Lonnie grabbed Margaret Ann and held her firmly against his chest with one arm. In his other hand was an open pocketknife, which he pointed at her throat. "You two are going to have to take a little ride with me."

Not realizing she was in mortal danger, Mam struggled against him. "Lonnie Williams, you let go of me! Who do you think you are?" She tried to bite his arm.

"Mam!" I shouted. "Stop! He's got a knife." I stared at the good-sized blade. He probably used it to slash our tire after we stopped. "It's a big knife."

"That's right." Lonnie's eyes were bloodshot. "And if she doesn't shut up, I'll slit her throat." Mam shut up. She looked at me, her eyes wide. I stepped back, away from Lonnie and Mam. "Stop. Don't move." He licked his lips. "You run or yell and she's dead."

I believed him. But my step had taken me to where I could see Bonnie flattened against the side of the truck. "I'm not going anywhere," I said loud enough for Bonnie to hear. "You've got the knife. And I'm not going to yell. Who'd hear me out here? Pinckney's two miles east, and the closest house is a mile or more behind those trees on the other side." Out of the corner of my eye, I saw Bonnie nodding. Now, I had to keep him talking long enough for her to escape. I tried to keep my voice calm. "Come on, Lonnie, let her go. We don't care if you're making meth. You can just take your stuff and leave us here. Take the keys. We won't be able to follow you. We won't tell anyone."

"Yeah, like this one ever shuts up. I been listening to her all week, and the only reason she's quiet now is me sticking this knife to her gizzard." He thrust the point of it under Mam's chin. "Feel that?"

"Don't hurt her, please," I said. Mam looked stricken as she shrank from the knife. "We'll do whatever you say. Just tell me what you want me to do."

I saw Bonnie hesitate, then realize this was no time for heroics. She rolled into the ditch on the other side and half ran, half crawled through the weeds, making for the woods. The purple sweatshirt blazed against the green and brown. Thank goodness Lonnie was focused on me.

"You shut up, too." Lonnie waved the knife at me. "Just shut up."
He was sweating. Two interfering females were not part of whatever
plan he'd hatched. I could almost see the wheels turning as he figured out what to do next. "Reach down and tie your shoelaces together," he told me. "Knot 'em tight. Then do the same with hers.
No funny business."

I did what he told me, double-knotting the laces. I had to shuffle
over to Mam and Lonnie. Maybe he wouldn't look too closely at hers,
but I couldn't take that chance. I felt her hand patting my hair for
comfort. Lonnie saw her and shoved me away with one foot. I toppled
over, then tried to stand with my shoes tied together.

"Get up!" he said. I used the bread truck's open door to hoist myself upright. Bonnie had disappeared into the woods. "Okay, now walk
back to my van." I let go of the truck door and stumbled. "I guess
you'll have to hop." He chuckled. "A bunny hop for Easter. We're right
behind you. No talking."

I longed to haul off and punch him, or at least spit in his face. But
with that knife pointed at Mam, I could only pray silently that Bonnie
would find help fast.

I hopped and shuffled. The Hired Killers sign had been taken off
the door.

"Go on to the back."

I looked behind me. Lonnie was dragging Mam with his arm under her chin. Her face was turning purple. "Look out! You're choking
her."

"Too bad," he said. But he did ease up on her throat. He didn't
want her dead. Yet. "Open the back door and get out that duct tape."

Duct tape. Oh, great. Mam's eyes were even wider. She really did
watch too much TV. I could see her fear and taste my own. My lip
was bleeding inside where I'd bitten it.

The duct tape was next to an open duffel bag. Behind it, up against
the metal grate separating the back of the van from the driver's seat,
the cockroach was lying on its back. The metal rod used to attach it to
its usual rooftop perch stuck straight up in the air.

Lonnie thrust Mam at me. "Put your hands behind your back," he told her. "You"—he motioned to me—"wrap her wrists together. Push up the sweatshirt first." I wound the tape as gently as I could, but Lonnie was peering over me. He had bad breath. "That's enough." He sliced the tape with the knife and pushed Mam inside the back of the van. She cried out in pain as her knee smashed against metal. "Didn't I tell you not to say anything?" He tore off a piece of duct tape and slapped it across her mouth. Her head snapped backward.

"Hold out your hands and put them together," Lonnie said. He quickly taped my wrists and clasped hands in front of me so I couldn't even move my fingers. I thought about trying to catch him under the chin with my fists, then maybe knee him in the groin, but he was too fast. Besides, my feet were tied together. Maybe if I didn't say anything, he'd forget about my mouth.

No such luck. I swallowed hard. If I started crying now, my nose would get stuffed and I wouldn't be able to breathe. Lonnie shoved me in the back of the van, lifting my legs so he could slam the door shut. It would have to be a cargo van with no rear or side windows. The only light came from the front, and it was partially blocked by the grate and that stupid cockroach.

Mam rolled next to me, and I pawed at her with my taped fists. My eyes were adjusting to the dimness. Where was Lonnie? Was he leaving in the bread truck? There was no sound of an engine. I scrambled to a sitting position but immediately ducked as Lonnie opened the driver's door. He tossed a sack on the seat and started the engine. I fell against the cockroach as he stomped on the gas and we jounced forward. I had a glimpse of the bread truck in the passenger-side mirror as we roared past. Mam was on her knees next to me looking, too, her bound arms awkwardly akimbo.

Just as we rounded a curve, the van rocked. *Boom!* A huge explosion came from behind us, bright light glinting off the mirrors and seeping through the cracks by the door.

Lonnie laughed maniacally as he accelerated. "Bye-bye, bread truck!"

CHAPTER TWENTY-ONE

Marsh Madness

Mam was taking the loss of the bread truck hard, shaking uncontrollably and blinking rapidly as tears rolled down her cheeks.

I didn't get it. If we ever got out of this mess, she wouldn't be the one explaining to the Finches that the truck they'd left in my care had blown sky high. I'd have to ask Bonnie if our car insurance or theirs covered meth explosions.

Bonnie! That's why Mam was having a fit. She thought her baby sister was still in the truck, or what was left of it.

How could I let her know Bonnie had escaped? I scooted toward her, my cheek banging on the rusty floor. Huddling close to her, I kept wiggling my eyebrows and nodding my head, trying to smile behind the wretched duct tape. She continued to sob. If she didn't quit soon, she'd hyperventilate. When we were little and Nanny put all three of us in the double bed in the cold middle room and piled heavy quilts on top of us, Mam had always insisted on pushing her head out so she could breathe—and talk. Bonnie and I preferred the warm, dark cocoon on either side of her. In fact, we used her back to draw pictures. "Cat!" Mam would call out, or "Heart!"

That gave me an idea. I pushed Mam over on her stomach, kneeing her to get her to focus. Then I used my fist to slowly trace the letters BOK on her back. She lifted her chin to look at me, clearly puzzled. BOK? I nodded, but she still didn't understand. I tried again, only this time I spelled BLT. When she nodded, I continued with OK. She went limp with relief. Bonnie Lynn Tyler was okay.

I looked up front. Lonnie was so intent on driving the dirt road that he hadn't noticed us squirming behind the grate and the palmetto bug. If I angled my head just so, I could see the side mirror. There was a blur of trees and brush, then something white. Was my life passing before my eyes? If so, it was going too fast. I thought of Mama and Daddy. And Will. Where was Will? Did he have any idea that the bug man was the drug man? Lonnie braked suddenly, and I fell against the cockroach, its wing digging into my side. Ouch! When the van reversed, then turned a corner, I glimpsed one of the Greek goddess statues. We were on the old road to the landing.

I turned to Mam, wondering if it was possible to communicate this with more hieroglyphics. She motioned her head to my left. The open duffel bag had shifted, a pair of athletic socks and a worn brown wallet spilling onto the van floor. I used my feet to push the wallet across the ridges, passing it off so Mam could kick it up under the bug out of sight. Wallet soccer. I wasn't sure what we could do with a wallet. A knife or something sharp would have been more useful. I rolled over to see what else was in Lonnie's luggage.

Just then, the van stopped and reversed again. Lonnie got out. I tensed, pulling away from the duffel bag and scrunching closer to Mam. We heard his footsteps. The back door flew open, and I blinked at the sudden light. If only we'd thought to spring out at him! But I saw the knife in his hand. There went Plan A. Plan B was Bonnie, but would she be able to find us? Maybe everybody would think we'd been blown up with the bread truck.

Lonnie scooped up the duffel bag. "Having fun, girlies?" He slammed the door and locked it.

I expected him to get back in the van, but instead there was the sound of clanking metal. The rear of the van sank a little, as if weight had been added. Lonnie was hitching up a trailer. Lord, I hoped it wasn't another meth lab.

Lonnie jumped back in the driver's seat and swung the van around. My stomach lurched. Now was not the time for me to get carsick. Lonnie backed down a steep incline, sending Mam and me sliding toward the rear door. The boat landing! The van shifted again. The boat was off the trailer now, completely in the water. It was a big boat, by the sound of the motor. Were we going with him?

The motor went silent. We strained our ears. Footsteps. He must have anchored the boat to a dock close by. The driver's door opened again. Lonnie reached across the seat to pick up his meth stash. "Don't want to forget this." He pressed his face against the grate. "Y'all have a nice swim. The tide's coming in right fast, so I expect it won't be long before this van is slippin' and slidin' right in the creek." He sounded gleeful. His face disappeared. I heard him release the emergency brake. The door slammed shut.

The boat motor started, and then its rumble faded. Lonnie was sailing solo.

This time, I was the one who went limp. I'd been trying so hard not to think about what Lonnie—Lonnie!—was going to do with us that all the things he could have done suddenly hit me. Compared to the alternatives, being tied up in a van was a good thing. We weren't sleeping with the fishes yet. But we needed a Plan C.

Mam flopped over on her stomach again. Did she want me to write on her back? No, she shoved her rear in the air and gestured with her bound hands at her back pocket. I could see something outlined against the denim. Her floral knife!

Her fingers were free enough to wield the knife, but she couldn't reach it because of her arms' position. And my taped fingers couldn't pick her pocket. She thrust her hands in the air, catching me on the chin. I felt her fingernails.

Yes, that was it! I pushed my face against her hands, and she clawed at my cheek, catching a corner of the duct tape. This was going to hurt. Better to get it over quick. As soon as she had a grip on the tape, I pulled back. The tape ripped away from my mouth. Well, I'd never need electrolysis.

"Thank you," I gasped. "Thank you, Lord. Thank you, Mam. And Bonnie really is fine. She's gone for help. She ran into the woods before he even put us in here." I licked my raw lips, tasting the tape's gummy residue and a metallic wetness.

Mam bobbed her head, then resumed wiggling her butt at me. The very top of the floral knife's handle was poking out of her pocket.

"Okay, Mam. I'm going to try and get your knife with my teeth 'cause my fingers are taped together." No go. I tried again, this time tugging on the fabric. Thank goodness for stretch jeans. My teeth chomped on the handle. I bit tightly and moved the knife over to Mam's wiggling fingers. She grabbed it.

"Smart girl," I said. "I know your fingers are numb, but you've almost got the sheath off. Be careful you don't cut yourself. If you sit up, you can saw my wrists better."

Mam clambered to her knees, the knife clutched between her fingers. She leaned her head back over her shoulder, trying to see.

"Just hold the knife still. I'll move my wrists." I pulled my arms apart as far as I could, but I still felt the blade nicking me. I sawed slowly but steadily. "It's starting to give a little."

The van shifted, and water lapped close by. Mam's fingers moved. "Look out!" I pulled my arms back. "You'll give me wrist scars. People will think I tried to kill myself." I felt the tape loosening more.

"There! You did it!" I pulled my hands free, flexing my fingers to get the circulation going. My wrists were raw from the tape and speckled with blood, but I didn't care. Water was seeping in the back of the van under the door. Once the water lifted the van, it wouldn't be long before the current caught it. Then it would tilt and sink.

"Do you want me to undo your mouth or your hands first?" Stupid question. I yanked the tape off her mouth.

"Ow! That hurt!"

"Tell me about it." I took the knife and began cutting her free.

"Hurry, Lindsey. We don't have much time. The floor's all wet.

We've got to get out of here."

"I know." I felt the tide lifting the van off the landing, the boat trailer dragging at the rear doors. "There. Untie your shoes." I fumbled with mine.

"You never were any good with knots." Mam had already untied her laces and tied them back. She stood, and her head hit the top of the van.

"Look out!" I caught her as she wobbled, and we both held onto the cockroach, which was sliding backward in the rising water. The brown wallet floated toward me. I shoved it in my back jeans pocket.

"There's a door." Mam pointed at the middle of the grate. "Come on. If we can make it to the front, maybe we can get out that way." She climbed over the cockroach and shimmied through the grate door.

"Don't open the driver's door!" Water rushing in there would throw the van off kilter. I tried to remember how to get out of a submerged vehicle. It all depended on which doors and windows were already open or could open. That was one of the reasons I hated electric windows, for all their convenience. If you rolled down a window in a hurry, you could squirm out to safety. Otherwise, you had to wait until the water pressure in the vehicle equaled that outside before you could open a door. Or something like that. Lonnie drove with his side window cracked but had made sure it was up when he abandoned us to the tide. He was lower than his blasted bug, which kept getting in my way.

"We need something to break the windshield." Mam kicked at it with her sneaker. No way was she waiting around for the van to fill with water. It already had reached the side windows. We'd have to go out the front.

"Here, try this." I stuffed the cockroach through the grate door. The water was coming in fast now. "That connector pole in its middle— it's metal."

I scrambled into the front seat with Mam and the bug. She had it by one wing. I grabbed the other.

"Together," Mam gasped. "One, two, three!"

We made only a slight crack in the glass. Still, it was a start. But we had to hurry. The van was listing to the left even as its rear end settled—shades of the *Titanic*.

"Again!" I slammed my half of the cockroach as hard as I could. The windshield shattered into pebbles of glass that rained into the water. I followed Margaret Ann out, crawling onto the hood.

"We're at Pinckney Landing." Mam tried to stand on the slippery surface, grabbing at me for support.

"Watch it, or we'll both be in the water."

"It's not that deep." Mam knelt and poked a foot in the water experimentally, still hanging onto my arm.

"The last time you said that, you disappeared."

"That was different. Look, you can see the ramp and the oyster shells."

The van moved again. The cockroach floated out the window by my feet. We couldn't stay here. "Be careful. Those oyster shells are like razors. And the current's really strong." I could see the gray-green water swirling, sucking at the van.

Mam slid gingerly off the hood on her rump, then stood. "Look, it's only to my knees. We're still on the ramp. Be careful, though. There's a lot of mud and slime. It's freezing, too."

No kidding. I slogged after Mam, shivering as the cold water molded my jeans to my legs. The salt water stung the scrapes I'd picked up along the way.

Mam stopped so suddenly I bumped into her back. She clutched my arm. "Shh," she said. "Look!"

I followed her eyes to the mud bank by the landing, where the creek spread into the reeds at high tide. The reeds were moving, but there wasn't any wind.

Mam's grip tightened. Was that gray-white shape lying in the ooze a cypress log? It looked more like . . . No, alligators were brownish green. This was just a cypress log. It wasn't moving.

Mam and I both jumped when the cypress log slithered into the creek with a gentle plop. Two red eyes stared at us before sinking into the water. Was it coming for us? No, the ripples indicated that the creature was moving away to our left, where Lonnie's cockroach floated on its back. I couldn't help it. A giggle burst from my throat. It was contagious. Mam laughed, too.

"Lindsey." Mam bent over, trying to catch her breath. "I can't believe it."

I looked at her, blinking back tears. "Me neither."

We clung to each other, gazing out at the creek. The palmetto bug was gone. So was the ghost gator.

"No one is going to believe we saw Turner's ghost gator." Mam leaned against a piling near the top of the landing, her chest heaving. "We did see it, didn't we?"

"Yep. And it attacked Lonnie's cockroach." I stomped my feet on the concrete ramp, trying to bring back feeling in my toes.

"He's a cockroach if there ever was one." Mam stomped her feet, too, as if she could crush him. "To think I trusted him to come into my house and look for termites. I wonder if I really have them. We'll have to get somebody else to come inspect now. I swear I hope that bug man rots in hell!"

"That's mighty strong language, missy, for Easter morning." The voice came from above us.

We looked up. There stood Marietta at the top of the landing in all her Easter glory. She was sporting a wide-brimmed hot-pink hat with white feathers gathered on the side. A hot-pink silk rose blossomed from the jacket lapel of her blindingly white silk suit. Her hands were on her hips, but I saw the concern in her eyes when she spotted our beat-up condition.

"Are y'all all right?" Bonnie appeared, panting at Marietta's side. She looked a picture, too—only more like us than Sunday-go-to-meeting. The knees of her jeans were ripped, her purple sweatshirt was daubed with dirt, and a long scratch ran from above her brow toward her ear. She must have torn through the woods to reach help so soon.

Mam, of course, was first. "We'll be okay. I thought you were blown up in the bread truck, only Lindsey wrote *BOK* on my back, and—"

"*BOK?*" Bonnie sounded like a crow with a cold.

I cut in. "Never mind. We'll explain later. How did you get here so fast? And how did you know where to come?"

"I ran into Marietta when I came out of the woods opposite where I went in. She was walking to Mount Zion, pretty as you please." Bonnie reached out her arm and pulled her sister up the landing, then held out the other arm to me.

"Marietta, we'll hug you when we get cleaned up," I said. "I'm not getting mud on that suit."

"This old thing?" Marietta pulled all three of us to her. She smelled of rose water. "I like to die when I seen Bonnie. Then she told me that Lonnie fellow put you in his van."

"It's a good thing I saw that before the bread truck exploded, or I'd have thought you were dead, too." Bonnie shuddered at the memory. "I saw the van head toward the goddesses, and when I told Marietta, she said if Lonnie was trying to leave Indigo in a hurry, he'd have a boat somewhere. Pinckney Landing was the closest place. We borrowed the nearest neighbor's car, told them to call 911, and here we are."

Marietta clucked over the three of us. "Y'all are a sight, for sure. Thank Jesus you alive. We need to get you into some dry clothes before you catch your death."

"We better stop by the bread truck first, or what's left of it," Bonnie said. "That's where everybody will be. Will or Olivia can get word to J. T. that you're all right, Mam. And they can send somebody after Lonnie."

Marietta hustled us forward. "Mr. Bennie's car's not much to look at, but it run good. Got a good heater, too. Bonnie, you turn it up high."

"Yes'm." Bonnie trotted ahead of us to the orange-brown El Dorado with whitewalls. "Ladies, your chariot awaits!"

CHAPTER TWENTY-TWO

No Place Like Home

" 'Swing low, sweet chariot,' " I hummed in the backseat. Thank goodness the El Dorado was carrying us home. I hardly noticed the seat springs poking into my thigh as Bonnie backtracked over the dirt roads.

"I think we can turn down the heat now." Mam leaned forward, sticking her head between the seats. An old wool blanket Marietta had found in the trunk was draped over our wet legs. It was beginning to smell like a farm animal. "Tell me honest, did y'all have any idea Lonnie was a bad guy?"

"Uh-uh." Bonnie swerved the land yacht to avoid a pothole. "My money was on Mike."

"Mike!" Mam was astounded. "But he's so nice."

"He has a yellow boat and bad teeth," Bonnie said. "Meth stains your teeth."

"So do other things," Mam said. "Mike got hit in the mouth when he was working on a yacht for some rich guy from out of state, and now he's fighting with the insurance company about how much he'll have to pay to get everything fixed. Teeth are expensive. I could have told you that if you asked."

"Sorry, it never occurred to me that you and Mike discussed dentistry." Bonnie slowed and looked around. "I guess it was Lindsey and me who talked about his teeth. Am I going the right way?"

"Turn left up there," I directed. "I never thought of Lonnie. He seemed so ordinary. But being a bug guy is good cover. He goes everywhere and knows who's home and who isn't. I bet he was who scared Cissy at Pinckney, and who Bonnie saw at the grate during the storm. I should have paid more attention to how he kept turning up. Only so did Turner."

"But Turner got shot at." Mam frowned.

"So he said, but maybe that was an old bullet hole." I shook my head. "Or maybe not. But Turner knows the back roads and creeks better than anyone but Posey."

"I hadn't thought of that." Mam twisted her hair. "Posey could be a drug runner."

"Land's sake!" Marietta turned on Mam. "You must have lost your mind, child, you think Posey have any truck with drugs."

"I didn't say he did, just that he could because he knows Pinckney and has a lot of local connections."

"The same could be said for everybody in this car," I said. Posey seemed an unlikely candidate for running an island cartel—the plantation took up all his time, for one thing. But I still wanted to ask him about Pinckney Plant sometime when Marietta wasn't around. "Lonnie was smart enough to make friends with everyone on Indigo without arousing suspicion."

Something besides a spring was jabbing me in the backside. What was I sitting on? Lonnie's wallet. I'd forgotten all about it.

"Let me see that." Mam grabbed it from my hand. "If there's any money in it, I think Lonnie owes me. He blew up my new Vera Bradley purse in the bread truck. You left yours in your car."

"You have to get a new license anyway," I pointed out. "And Clinique's having a special, so you can get new makeup. And you just got the purse this morning. What else was in there?"

"My cell phone, so J. T. can't reach me now. What time is it, anyway?"

"A little after ten," Bonnie said. "But I don't think you're going to make it to the eleven o'clock service."

"We done praised the Lord already for saving your skin from that devil in disguise." Marietta dabbed her face with a lace hanky. "Do turn that heat down, Bonnie."

"J. T.'s taking my arrangement to the Episcopal church," Mam said. "He won't even miss me till I don't turn up next to him and Cissy at our service. That was something else in my purse—my Easter offering, although J. T. can put something in the collection plate. Cissy's picture from the Valentine's dance was in my wallet, too, but of course she was with Jimmy, and we don't need any more reminders. Maybe I'll get Lucille to cut my hair before I have to get my new license picture. Let's see what Lonnie's looks like, the scumbag." She scowled at the laminated card, then peered closer. "Hey, look, Lonnie's not Lonnie. I mean, it's Lonnie's picture, but it says this guy is Purvis Spivey. Well, I guess if you're going to change your name, you ought to improve it."

"Hey, let me see that." I looked at the license. It was from Tennessee and had expired two years ago. "Bonnie, do you remember when Miss Maudie was talking about Lorna having no people? Didn't she say her husband had a cousin from Tennessee he went to prison with?"

"Uh, that sounds right. I think she said it was for drugs."

The pieces were beginning to fall into place. Lorna was married to a Spivey. He had a cousin who was into drugs. Lonnie had been at the Gatortorium. And Lonnie had been first on the scene—after me—when Scott went into the marsh. It was my turn to stick my head into the front seat. "Bonnie, if Lonnie has a license for a Purvis Spivey, that can't be a coincidence."

"Hold that thought." Bonnie slowed as we came around a curve. "It looks like the whole island is skipping church to look at the bread-truck crumbs."

It was Sunset Court all over again—orange cones, the Haz-Mat team, fire trucks, sheriff's cars. EMS, too. Where was Will?

Bonnie tried to honk the El Dorado's horn, but it barely bleated. She banged the steering wheel in frustration. "I kept trying to honk the horn when we were driving up to you at the landing, hoping you'd know help was on the way."

"It's just as well." Mam leaned forward again. "You might have scared off the ghost gator."

Bonnie turned around, and Marietta's hat swiveled at the same time. "What ghost gator?"

"You get bumped on the head, child?"

"No, yes . . . Well, that was in the van." Mam touched her forehead. "And the hail the other night. But we really did see the ghost gator. Tell them, Lindsey."

"You tell them," I said, opening the car door. "Olivia, over here!" When I had to, I could yell as loud as Mam.

Olivia came running. "Are y'all okay? Is Margaret Ann in there? I've got to let the major know right away. He's over at White's Landing with the DEA. They sent boats out looking for y'all and Lonnie as soon as we got the call he had you hostage. They called the Coast Guard, too, for the helicopter."

"Olivia, tell them Lonnie left from Pinckney, heading toward the open water, we think. But Olivia, Lonnie's not Lonnie. We think his real name is Purvis Spivey."

Her eyebrows shot up as she made the connection. "I'm on it. You need EMS?"

"No, just dry clothes," I said.

"Well, the road's blocked here 'cause of those meth fumes. Go on back to Pinckney. I'll tell the major you're there." She sprinted off toward her cruiser.

"Well?" Bonnie asked. "What did you find out?"

"That pretty much every law-enforcement agency is on Lonnie's tail. And that we can't go through here."

"So where do we go?" Mam's voice was plaintive.

"Where you think?" Marietta's voice was firm. "Pinckney."

"Here, Lindsey, you get the Pinckney purple one." Mam held out a tour-guide costume to me.

We all three were in the hall bathroom, dressed only in our skivvies. Marietta had taken away our wet clothes for washing. If she'd had her way, she'd have plunked all of us in Miss Augusta's claw-foot tub upstairs and scrubbed the pluff mud—and the skin—right off us. As it was, she'd shaken her head as she handed us clean towels. "That's a whore's bath you're taking," she'd said. "Be sure and use hot water. I'll go find you some clothes."

"Thank goodness our underwear's not wet," Bonnie said. "She'd put us in pantaloons. Are those Victoria's Secret panties, Mam? I like them."

"You should. You gave them to me for Christmas." Mam hiked up her bra strap. "Like Mama says, always wear good underwear in case you're in an accident. But I don't think she meant this kind of accident."

"This would be a hard one to anticipate." I pulled a brush through my hair. I kept some toiletries at Pinckney, but not extra clothes. That was going to change. "Who'd have thunk the Finches' bread truck was a meth lab?"

"Don't you know Lonnie had a fit when he saw it was gone." Bonnie was dabbing some concealer on the scratch on her face. "I still can't get over him being a drug kingpin. Did Will say anything about accomplices when he called, Lindsey?"

I grinned. "He said—surprise, surprise—that several of the Smoaks were helping him with his inquiries. You know, Lonnie could have met some of them in prison. There's always at least one doing time for something. They haven't found Lonnie yet, but they've got every landing from Hilton Head to Georgetown under surveillance. He's considered armed and dangerous."

Just how dangerous kept coming back to me. Going over events with Will, I'd realized the only reason Lonnie hadn't blown us up with the bread truck was that he needed hostages until he got off the island. Once he was in the boat, he'd left us in the van to drown. Of course, we didn't know he'd already killed once to protect his drug dealing. And he didn't know that we had his old wallet with his ID in it. Otherwise, he might have slit our throats before putting out to sea."

Mam took the brush from me. "I still can't get over Lonnie being Lorna's cousin-in-law and killing her because she recognized him. I guess he figured she'd jeopardize his meth operation, or maybe she threatened to blackmail him and wanted in on the profits. Lindsey, I wouldn't kill you for that, and you're my blood cousin. I mean, I'd try to get you some help first. Maybe I'd pay you off, but I wouldn't poison you."

"Gee, thanks—I think. More victims are killed by people they know than by strangers. I bet he was as surprised to see her as she was him. She knew he wasn't any Lonnie Williams. Imagine just running into each other at the Gatortorium—'Of all the gin joints in all the world . . .' It's not like Indigo Island is Grand Central Station. And then he framed Scott. I wonder how he found out Scott was the stalker. Lonnie didn't seem that smart."

Bonnie turned to the pile of tour-guide costumes Marietta had brought us. "He was lucky—at least until he ran into us."

"We're lucky, too." I shivered, remembering the amoral gleam in Lonnie's eyes, his round face sneering. Dr. Jekyll and Mr. Hyde. "He didn't look like a killer until the end."

"Most don't wear signs." Bonnie was being the pragmatic lawyer. "A killer is anybody who kills."

Mam was examining the hole in her hair in the mirror. "I wonder where the real Lonnie is. Do you suppose he got killed, too? At the least, he's a victim of identity theft, like me."

"Lonnie Williams was a good name to choose." Bonnie shook out a guide dress to check its length. "There are so many Williams families in the Low Country, you'd just assume he was from around here. 'Bout the only place there aren't a passel of Williams is Williams. It's full of Warrens."

Mam and I nodded. The crossroads community near Walterboro

should have been renamed Warren by now.

I looked at Bonnie in her getup. "Are they all purple?"

"Yep," she said. "I think Miss Augusta has a standing order at Wal-Mart."

"I'm not wearing a hoop skirt." Mam smoothed the dress she'd slipped over her head. "No one's going to see us anyway. We don't have any shoes either."

"Miss Augusta's probably got some footies in a drawer, if you're worried about your tootsies," I said. "And if you need a hat, there's always the Gloria Swanson turban with that rhinestone in the center."

Mam surveyed herself in the mirror. "I think this outfit calls for some bling bling."

"It calls for something." Bonnie sighed. "I sure hope Cissy brings us decent clothes as soon as she gets out of church." She looked at her watch. "It's going on noon. I don't see why we can't just wait in here until our real clothes dry or Cissy gets here. It's not like anyone is going to show up at Pinckney right when it opens. And aren't the regular guides on duty today?"

"Not till one," I said. "I'd planned to hold the fort until then, so everyone could go to church. Come on, let's go sit on the porch. It'll be warm in the sun."

We trooped through the parlor and opened the heavy front door. Sunlight spilled across the brick courtyard. The azaleas looked sad, to say the least. But they'd come back. They were survivors, like us. That reminded me. "Y'all, what are we going to do about Lorna?" I asked. "MaryMar's gone flitting off with Ron. Who knows when she'll be back or what she'll want to do about a funeral?"

"She'll be back, if only to see whether Lorna left her anything." Bonnie sat in the swing.

"According to MaryMar, Lorna didn't have a pot to pee in," Mam said, leaning against a column. "MaryMar—or Ron—is probably going to have to foot the bill to bury her. Remember, she has no people."

I sat next to Bonnie. "We could be her people for a memorial service. And we can share some of ours."

"That's a good idea. Our mamas and their circles all love a good funeral." Mam joined us on the swing, elbowing her way into the middle. "I'll call the funeral parlor tomorrow and see if we can set up a memorial service. I can do the flowers. Miss Maudie will want to come, and Aunt Cora's back tomorrow, too."

"Mam, if you're going to sit, sit," I said. "Don't swing. I've floated enough today."

For once, she was quiet. We all were, lost in our thoughts. Bonnie was probably thinking about welcoming her boys back. Mam was most likely mentally going over the guest list for the memorial service. I was looking forward to seeing Will later. His voice had been warm on the phone, and there'd been no I-told-you-so's. We were both too independent—muleheaded, Mam would say—for us not to have some adjustment issues. Meanwhile, March was almost behind us, and April in Paris had nothing on April on Indigo. Sitting here in the sun was a reminder of the spring ahead, with its honeysuckle-kissed air and promise of the future. After all that had happened lately, the peace was refreshing.

It didn't last long. A shiny black Cadillac—it looked like the newest model—was speeding up the winding drive. Whoever it was knew the way, dodging every oak.

We stood as the car halted in front of the steps. The driver's door opened, and a familiar figure got out. Posey! But where had he gotten the car?

He waved up to us, smiling, as he strolled to open the passenger door. We looked at each other, then at the ebony cane emerging from the car. It was followed by a foot clad in a vintage high heel. Next came the unmistakable red head.

"I declare!" said Bonnie.

"Dad-gum!" said Mam.

"Welcome home, Miss Augusta," I said. "Welcome to Pinckney Plantation."

Epilogue

On the last night of March, a breeze rustled the Bottle Tree standing sentinel in the marsh. Glass tinkled like wind chimes, and streamers, their color drained by darkness, floated on the air.

The big, empty house nearby slept quietly, shadowed by pines, palmettos, and live oaks. Spanish moss drifted from heavy limbs, where migratory birds settled in for a rest. A lone light shone in an outbuilding. Someone kept late hours.

The gentle breeze touched the tidal creek, stirring sweet grass and spartina. Crickets chirped. Frogs burped. A silver cypress log lay in the mud. And the ghost gator awakened once more.

Acknowledgments

Marsh Madness is a work of fiction. You won't find Pinckney Plantation, Indigo Island, or Granville County on any map of the South Carolina Low Country. Like the characters in the book, they are products of our imagination. Where actual place names occur in the narrative, they have been used fictitiously.

Many family members and friends helped us in the writing of "the second book." We would especially like to thank our parents, Frances and Donald Pate and Boodie and Robert Godwin; first readers Kathy Roe, Rebecca Swain Vadnie, and Aly Greer; the Edisto Island Historical Society; Bruce and Tecla Earnshaw of Cassina Point Plantation; Ted Clamp and Heyward Clamp of the Edisto Island Serpentarium; Nancy's friends at the *Orlando Sentinel*; the florists, wedding planners, and brides with whom Meg and Gail work; the Reverend Stanley and Sarahjane LaTorre, owners of the real bread truck; Katy Miller; Ed Malles; Nancy Lassiter; Patti Morrison; Jackie and Suzy Sanderson; Watson Johnson; the Cheese Club of Grater Orlando; Deputy Eric Hampton, Orange County Sheriff's Office; Greg Odom, Home Free

Pest Control; our "mystery mom," Kathy Hogan Trocheck; and the entire staff of John F. Blair, Publisher. Thanks, too, to the many readers, booksellers, and librarians who helped make our first novel, *Fiddle Dee Death*, such a success. You are our people.

Caroline Cousins is a pseudonym for Nancy Pate and her "one-and-a-half-times" first cousins, sisters Meg Herndon and Gail Greer. (Their mothers are sisters, and their fathers are first cousins.) Nancy, former longtime book critic for the *Orlando Sentinel*, lives in Orlando, Florida. Meg, an independent wedding florist, and Gail, a designer for a floral preservation business and a former plantation tour guide, live in Mount Pleasant, South Carolina. The trio's first book was *Fiddle Dee Death*.